Sierra Stories

True Tales of Tahoe

Volume 2

Cover design and layout by —
Riley Works
Tahoe City, CA

Mic Mac
Publishing

P. O. Box 483 • Carnelian Bay, CA 96140

Sierra Stories

True Tales of Tahoe

Volume 2

by

Mark McLaughlin

For one who knows
this country.

Mark
McLaughlin
Nov.
1998

Acknowledgments

No book is created in a vacuum. I thank the following people for their time and assistance.

- Phillip I. Earl, Lee Mortensen and Lee Brumbaugh, of the Nevada Historical Society.

- Guy Louis Rocha, State Archivist, Nevada State Library and Archives, Carson City.

- The friendly staff at the Getchell Library of the University of Nevada, Reno.

- William B. Berry, Sierra Ski Historian, and at 95 years of age, the oldest working newspaperman in North America.

- Ellen Harding, of the California State Library, California History Room.

- Eileen Kessler, at the Nevada State Library.

- Steven Staiger, of the Palo Alto Historical Association.

- Dohn Riley, of Riley Works, for his critical eye, both in format and text.

Dedication

To my family, friends and colleagues, for all their
support and encouragement.

And to the brave pioneers, who showed great courage
and determination.

About the Author

Historian Mark McLaughlin is an award-winning nonfiction writer who lives on Lake Tahoe's North Shore. A popular lecturer, Mark teaches Sierra Nevada history using dramatic stories, slide shows and field trips.

Mark has authored more than one hundred articles in regional and national publications. His weekly column *Sierra Stories* can be read in the local *North Tahoe-Truckee Week* magazine. He also writes *Weather Window*©, a feature column which appears in Truckee and North Shore newspapers.

Sierra Stories: True Tales of Tahoe (Volume 1), was a 1997 regional bestseller.

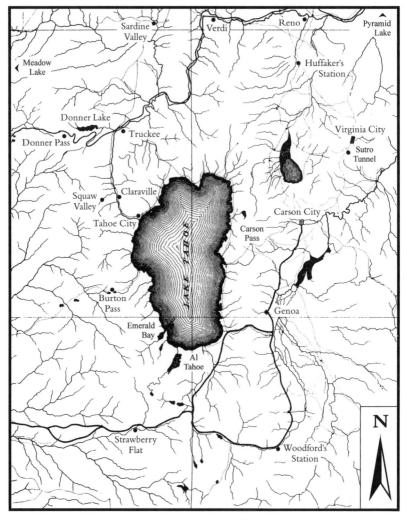

1 inch equals approximately 11 miles

" Go West, young man, and
grow up with the country. "

— *Horace Greeley, 1857*

Contents

Sarah Wallis: California's First Feminist.................. 3

Black Bart: Sierra Stage Robber 15

Battle at Pyramid Lake 23

Nancy Kelsey: 1st White Woman over the Sierra .. 37

Twain on Tahoe 51

Alice Hartley: The Madness of Meadow Lake 65

Julia Bulette: Queen of D Street.......................... 77

Captain Barter: Hermit of Emerald Bay 85

The Vision of Crazy Sutro 97

Sam Brown & Tom Bell: Sierra Bad Men.......... 109

Sarah Wallis: California's First Feminist

THEY WERE THE VANGUARD of the greatest human migration in American history. Best known as the Stephens-Murphy-Townsend Party of 1844, this small band of hardy pioneers had challenged the unknown and survived. Lured by the promise of a mild climate, few diseases, and the open, fertile land of California, these pioneers had chosen to risk their lives in an overland crossing to the Pacific Ocean. There were only fifty emigrants in the Stephens Party, of which sixteen were children. These indefatigable families battled rough country and extreme weather as they pushed and pulled their heavily-laden wagons more than two thousand miles. They marched all the way from Council Bluffs, Missouri, across the rugged Rocky Mountains at South Pass, through the harsh Nevada desert and then up and over the storm-swept Sierra Nevada. Their epic journey took them nearly a year, but they became the first wagon train to breach the Sierra and open the long-sought California Trail.

Little known among these daring Argonauts was a quiet, unassuming young woman. Sarah had braved the dangerous transcontinental crossing with the Stephens Party. She too had nearly starved when the pioneers were trapped for weeks, snowbound along the headwaters of the Yuba River.

Sarah Armstrong was an eighteen-year-old newlywed from Ohio when she and her husband, Allen Montgomery, joined other California-bound settlers in Missouri. Although the move west was her husband's decision, Sarah was hoping for a better life in the West, far from the dreary farm life of her youth. In the small Midwestern farming communities of 1844, there was a strict division of labor and a woman's work was in the household. Wives were expected to make and repair clothing, do all the cooking, and care for the children. But men were not the real "breadwinners" of this economy. Besides their regular domestic chores, women also generated one-third to one-half of all the food production on the farm. In addition to cultivating gardens, during harvest, wives would likely be out in the fields helping the men. One contemporary doctor commented on the conditions of farmwomen; "In the civilization of the nineteenth century, a farmer's wife, as a general rule, is a laboring drudge. It is safe to say, that on three farms out of four, the wife works harder and endures more than the husband and more than the farm-hand."

Besides all the hard work, married women in the nineteenth century enjoyed no civil rights; wives could not vote, own property, serve on juries, or hold public office. Husbands were recognized by law as the head of the household. Men even owned their wives' labor power; any wages that a woman earned while married were legally owed to her husband. In general, few women agreed with the idea of moving west, away from their family and friends. One young midwestern girl wrote in her diary, "I came in one evening to see a look on dear mother's face that I had never seen before. I walked away after the usual greeting and sat silent. After a time she said, "What do you think your father has done? He has sold the farm and as soon as school closes, we are moving to California."

The trip across the plains fulfilled Allen Montgomery's male fantasy of camaraderie, action, and achievement. Initially, young Sarah may have been reluctant to join her husband on the trail, but remaining home with no independent livelihood was a poor prospect. On the trail, their chores would be different, but still split by gender. Men were primarily concerned with transportation. They were responsible for the care of wagons and livestock, as well as for the leadership and protection of the family. The daily march usually began just after sunrise and did not stop until the midday meal, which the women had usually prepared that morning. After an hour or so of rest, the party resumed the trek west until late afternoon when the men were so tired they could barely walk.

The men worked at peak capacity from the time the oxen were yoked in the morning until they were herded in the evening. But when the wagons were parked and the oxen set out to graze, the men were off duty. They could work at their own leisure, rest, and enjoy the company of the other men. For women like Sarah, however, there was no relief from the daily drudgery of their endless chores. They awoke at 4 a.m., an hour before the men, in order to stoke the fire and prepare breakfast. One man observed in the pre-dawn darkness, "…other than the women busy cooking breakfast, there was no activity except sleeping, which is performed by the male part of the camp to the greatest perfection." During the day, Sarah and the other women gathered sagebrush or buffalo dung, adding miles to their daily trek.

When the wagons stopped for the day, the women went to work. For men, the evening was the reward for a hard day's work; for Sarah and the other women, it was four to five hours of additional labor. One female diarist wrote, "To ride on horseback, rain or shine, tired or sick, or whatever might be the matter, then as soon as we get into camp, go to work!" In addition to their daily cooking chores, women also prepared butter and cheese, boiled potatoes and then mashed them, made gravies, stewed dried fruit, made bread and biscuits; they even made preserves from wild berries gathered along the trail.

Despite all the hardships on the trail, the pioneers in petticoats made the best of it. One humorous frontier aphorism summed up the women's overland experience perfectly: "This country is all right for men and dogs, but it's hell on women and horses." The transcontinental crossing may have been tough on Sarah Montgomery, but her early days in California proved as difficult as any of those years on the farm. Shortly after Sarah and Allen arrived at Sutter's Fort in 1845, Captain John Sutter ordered them north to work, hand-sawing timber into badly needed lumber. The Montgomery's built themselves a small, one-room cabin near Sutter Creek and settled in. Life for pioneer women in early California was lonely and isolated. Their endless duties and the long distances between settlements gave American women few opportunities to visit one another.

But Sarah envisioned a better life for women and she was ready to act on it. In January 1846, Sarah organized California's first quilting-bee party. Nearly twenty women attended, a surprising number considering the difficulty of winter travel in those days. The lonely women sewed, talked and laughed late into the night. Sarah wondered how she could do more.

Raised on a farm, Sarah had had little formal education, but she was very ambitious. When her husband joined in the Bear Flag Rebellion in 1846, she moved back to Sutter's Fort to attend school. She listened in on children's classes in order to learn how to read and write. She remained there until the spring of 1847, when Allen marched home from the war. Unfortunately, after all the thrills and adventure of war and battle, Allen had grown bored with married life. Later that year, Allen deserted Sarah and sailed for Honolulu, leaving her alone and penniless.

Two years later, Sarah married Talbot Green, a prominent, wealthy merchant in San Francisco. Talbot Green was
generous and well-liked, but also somewhat mysterious. He
had emigrated to California on horseback with the Bidwell-
Bartleson Party of 1841. Talbot had held the position of President of that party, ranked between Captain John Bartleson
and Secretary John Bidwell. At that time he had carried medical supplies and acted as a doctor. Green had also packed a
heavy bag of metal that he claimed was lead for rifle-balls.

Respected now and wealthy, Sarah loved Talbot Green and
her new life in San Francisco. It was a long way from the farm
and her times with Allen Montgomery. By 1851, Sarah was
pregnant with her first child. But when her husband ran for
mayor of San Francisco, a shady past was discovered. Green
was publicly denounced as Paul Geddes, a fugitive bank clerk
from Pennsylvania, who had deserted his wife and children a
decade earlier. Presumably the bag of "lead" he had hauled
across the continent was gold bullion stolen from the Pennsylvania bank. Labeled a bigamist and a scoundrel, Talbot
Green vehemently denied the accusations. Vowing to clear
his name, he shipped out for the East Coast. A large crowd of
San Franciscans cheered the popular businessman as they escorted him to the pier. Six months pregnant, Sarah grimly
watched her husband go. Geddes would never return, but to
his credit, he did send money to Sarah to care for their son.
Green later wrote his business partner, Thomas O. Larkin,
and admitted his guilt.

Within a short time Sarah Montgomery Green was granted
a divorce. In order to make ends meet she cooked and took in
boarders. In 1854, at age 29, and with a young son to raise,
she married Joseph Wallis, her third husband. Wallis, a well-
known attorney and popular politician from Santa Clara
County, was appointed judge and then later elected as a state

senator. It wasn't long before Sarah herself began getting involved in politics. The success of that first quilting bee long ago had enforced her desire to shed the social shackles that constrained Victorian women. In 1856, Sarah bought the beautiful, 250-acre Mayfield Farm, in present-day Palo Alto. To take title in her own name was highly unusual for a woman in the early west, but there was nothing ordinary about Sarah Wallis. She had become a vigorous force in the social and civic life of Mayfield.

Sarah Wallis championed many causes for her community and California. She spearheaded a successful effort to bring a railroad line from San Francisco through Mayfield. The grateful citizens of Mayfield thanked Sarah with a banquet in her honor. Top officials of Southern Pacific Railroad and Senator Leland Stanford attended the celebrated event. Later Sarah started California's first Women's Club. The influence she wielded was extraordinary at a time when women were shut out of politics. Wallis persistently lobbied the California Legislature in Sacramento for women's rights. Sarah led protests demanding a woman's right to vote, to own title on real property, access to state colleges, and the right for women to practice law. Outspoken women were often ridiculed in the 19th century as their protests fell on deaf ears in the male-dominated government and business communities. Ever circumspect, western historian, Hubert H. Bancroft, described her unorthodox activist behavior as "taking part in public meetings of progressive and strong-minded females."

The Wallis' built a large, elegant house and surrounded it with fruit orchards, trees and flowers. Using her home as a base, Sarah aggressively asserted her agenda for women's rights. In 1870, she was elected president of the California Women's Suffrage Association. Her prominence in the 19th century women's movement grew to such height that Susan B. Anthony, as well as President Ulysses S. Grant, visited her in Mayfield. Leland Stanford's wife, Elizabeth Cady Stanton, wrote, "The most successful meetings ever held in Santa Clara County have been at Mayfield."

During her lifetime, Sarah gave birth to five children, including her first son by Talbot Green. Talbot H. Wallis later became the California State Librarian in Sacramento. For a time, Sarah owned the land where General Sutter built his mill. It was on that site that James Marshall would later discover the yellow flakes that sparked the California Gold Rush. Sarah Wallis was 87 years old when she died on January 11, 1905. She had been wealthy once, but through her generosity had spent most of her money helping others. Surprisingly, there are no known photographs of Sarah Wallis. Sarah was buried in an unmarked grave beside her husband and son in the Union Cemetery in Redwood City, California. Today, the only monument to her energy, vision and influence is a little-known state historic plaque near the site of her beautiful Mayfield House, which was destroyed by fire in 1936.

Although Sarah Wallis died six years before women won the right to vote in California, her persistent battle for equal opportunity was for all women, not just for herself. In 1844, members of the Bidwell–Bartleson Party were the first Caucasians to stand on the shore of Lake Tahoe and the first to bring wagons over the Sierra. This early feminist with little schooling had not only helped open the California Trail, but she blazed a life–long path for all women.

HOMESITE OF SARAH WALLIS
MAYFIELD FARM

SARAH ARMSTRONG WALLIS (1825-1905) WAS A PIONEER IN
THE CAMPAIGN FOR WOMEN'S VOTING RIGHTS. IN 1870 SHE
WAS ELECTED PRESIDENT OF CALIFORNIA'S FIRST STATEWIDE
SUFFRAGE ORGANIZATION WHICH IN 1873 INCORPORATED AS
THE CALIFORNIA STATE WOMAN SUFFRAGE EDUCATION
ASSOCIATION. THE HOME SHE BUILT ON THIS SITE, MAYFIELD
FARM WAS A CENTER OF SUFFRAGE ACTIVITIES ATTRACTING
STATE AND NATIONAL LEADERS SUCH AS SUSAN B. ANTHONY,
ELIZABETH CADY STANTON AND ULYSSES S. GRANT.

CALIFORNIA REGISTERED
HISTORICAL LANDMARK NO.969

PLAQUE PLACED BY THE STATE DEPARTMENT OF PARKS AND
RECREATION IN COOPERATION WITH THE WOMEN'S HERITAGE MUSEUM
OF PALO ALTO AND THE CITY OF PALO ALTO. OCTOBER 11, 1986.

CHAPTER TWO SELECTED SOURCES

Horace S. Foote, *Pen Pictures from the Garden of the World, Santa Clara,* The Lewis Publishing Co., Chicago, Illinois, 1888.

Frederic Hall, *History of San Jose and Surroundings with Biographical Sketches of Early Settlers,* Bancroft & Co., San Francisco, California, 1871.

Eugene T. Sawyer, *History of Santa Clara California with Biographical Sketches,* Historic Record Company, Los Angeles, California, 1922.

Pamela Gullard & Nancy Lund, *History of Palo Alto: The Early Years,* Scottwall Associates, San Francisco, California, 1989.

Cathy Luchetti & Carol Olwell, *Women of the West,* The Library of the American West, Orion Books, New York, NY, 1982.

Lillian Schlissel, *Women's Diaries of the Westward Journey,* Schocken Book, New York, NY, 1982.

Glenda Riley, *Women and Indians on the Frontier, 1825 – 1915,* University of New Mexico Press, Albuquerque, New Mexico, 1984.

Elizabeth Margo, *Women of the Gold Rush*, Indian Head Books, New York, NY, 1955.

William W. Fowler, *Women on the American Frontier*, Corner House Publishers, Williamstown, Massachusetts, 1985.

Kenneth L. Holmes, *Covered Wagon Women - Diaries & Letters from the Western Trails, 1840 – 1849, Volume I,* University of Nebraska Press, Lincoln, Nebraska, 1983.

Susan Armitage & Elizabeth Jameson, *The Women's West,* University of Oklahoma Press, Norman, Oklahoma, 1987.

Donovan Lewis, *Pioneers of California: True Stories of Early Settlers in the Golden State,* Scottwall Associates, San Francisco, California, 1993.

San Francisco Chronicle, January 15, 1905.

Black Bart: Sierra Stage Robber

I T TOOK WESTERN LAWMEN eight long years to nab the most noted of all 19th century Sierra stagecoach robbers. Time enough for the legendary "Black Bart" to pull off a record twenty-eight hold-ups. Bart's reign of terror lasted the better part of a decade because no one could identify the mysterious lone bandit who dared waylay Wells Fargo stages all by himself. Bart was a most improbable highwayman. He was skinny, short and bald, and didn't even own a horse. He walked to his crimes, carrying a shotgun so old and rusty that it wouldn't shoot. In fact, the weapon was never loaded.

Black Bart always worked alone, although he would frequently create decoy gunmen for back-up, placing wooden sticks on boulders to stimulate their rifles. Bart's strategy was deceptively simple psychology. He would wait at a dangerous bend in the road where the stage was forced to creep along slowly. At just the right moment, he emerged as an apparition in the deepening twilight. To enhance his supernatural qualities, Bart wore a long white linen duster over his clothes. A ghostly flour sack covered his head and derby hat, with two holes cut out for eye slits. In a "deep and hollow voice" Bart would command the trembling stagecoach driver to "Throw down the box!" Drivers knew that he meant the valuable Wells Fargo security chest. For stage drivers in the mountains, Bart's spooky reputation unnerved the most stoic of them. In order to further his ruse, Bart would often call out to his imaginary gang, "If he dares to shoot, give him a solid volley, boys!"

Bart was considered a gentleman by most of his victims; his focus seemed to be the Wells Fargo money box and the U.S. Mail. Well-known as an extremely courteous bandit, Bart refused to steal women's jewelry and avoided gun play at all costs. Some people sympathized with Black Bart. California, like much of the United States, was in the grip of a severe economic depression in the 1870s. The powerful Bank of California collapsed in August 1875, taking with it many financial institutions and businesses. At the same time, mining stocks plummeted on the San Francisco Stock Exchange. Drought forced thousands of farmers and farm laborers to seek work in the cities. There were ten thousand hungry workingmen on public relief in San Francisco alone; other men were fighting for jobs that paid only two dollars a day. Crime replaced industry, and the decade became known as the "Era of Good Stealing." Between November 1870 and November 1884, the total amount taken from Wells Fargo by stage robbers, train bandits, and burglars was in excess of $415,000.

Black Bart was not the first man to rob a California stagecoach; that bold deed was accomplished in 1856 by Tom Bell. Bart's life of crime began July 1875, when he held up a Wells Fargo express stage with a double-barreled shotgun. No one was hurt, but Bart's booty was $300 in gold coin. Unlike other road agents, Black Bart was patient. He did not strike again until the following summer, when he robbed another stage near Quincy, California. It was a modest start, but the seemingly insignificant, random hold-ups were only the beginning of Black Bart's legacy. For the next eight years, Bart pulled heists from Shasta, in the north, to Fort Ross on the Sonoma coast, but he preferred to haunt the Wells Fargo stage routes throughout the Sierra Nevada gold country. He never fired a shot and always got the "box."

In his fourth robbery, Bart wrote a short poem which he left in the cleaned out money box. He signed the note "Black Bart – The PO8." Evidently, Bart considered his short rhyming missives to be "PO8ry." After his fifth hold-up, the poet laureate of road agents wrote the last poem he would leave at the scene of a crime:

> Here I lay me down to sleep
> To await the coming morrow
> Perhaps success, perhaps defeat
> And everlasting sorrow.
>
> Let come what will, I'll try it on
> My condition can't be worse
> And if there's money in that box
> 'Tis munny in my purse.

Wells Fargo detectives said that the handwriting proved the "Black Bart" bandit had extensive experience in clerical work and declared that they would find the cocky criminal soon. An $800 reward was posted for Black Bart's arrest and conviction. Despite this incentive and a well-organized search by Wells Fargo's Chief of Detectives, James B. Hume, Bart began to steal with impunity. He seemed to be everywhere. Black Bart had a unique ability to travel extraordinary distances in impossibly short periods of time. J.B. Hume could barely keep up with the widely-scattered hold-ups. At least Bart acted like a gentleman. In order to calm their passengers, the Wells Fargo Company published a statement about the bandit's *modus operandi*; "He has never manifested any viciousness and there is reason to believe he is averse to taking human life. He is polite to all passengers, and especially to ladies. He comes and goes from the scene of the robbery on foot; seems to be a thorough mountaineer and a good walker." By

1883, Black Bart had become a romantic legend in California, but his luck was about to change.

The morning of November 3, 1883, dawned clear and cold.
Reason McConnell, driver for the Nevada Stage Company,
was hauling nearly five
thousand dollars in gold
dust and coin. His
only passenger was
nineteen-year-old
Jimmy Rolleri,
who was keeping
McConnell
company on the
ride over Funk
Hill, near the
Stanislaus
River. The
horse-drawn
carriage slowed
as it climbed the
ridge, and Jimmy
jumped off. He
had his Henry rifle
and wanted to see if
he could shoot a rabbit,
or a deer if he was lucky.
The horses slowly plodded up
the steep grade, until, just before the crest, Black Bart appeared
out of the bushes. Bart had been here before. He had committed his first robbery at this very spot on July 26, 1875.

Black Bart ordered McConnell to throw down the gold
box, but this time the Wells Fargo chest was bolted to the
floor of the stagecoach. While Bart took an axe to the lock on

the box, Jimmy Rolleri quietly emerged from the brush. When the road agent backed out of the coach holding a heavy sack of gold and a bundle of mail, Jimmy and his trusty rifle were waiting for him. As soon as he saw the armed teenager, Bart dove into the underbrush and ran for his life. McConnell grabbed Jimmy's gun and fired two shots at the fleeing bandit. Both rounds missed. At that Jimmy said, "Here, let me shoot. I'll get him, and I won't kill him, either." Jimmy's bullet hit Bart in the hand, forcing him to drop the mail, but the fleet-footed thief disappeared into the thicket still carrying the sack of gold. Bart stashed the loot, tramped one hundred miles through rugged, overgrown country in three days, and then boarded an eastbound train for Reno to hide out. Later in the week, he returned to California.

Black Bart may have escaped, but this time he left incriminating evidence behind, most damaging of which was a handkerchief with a San Francisco laundry mark on it. Exhaustive detective work by Harry N. Morse, ex-sheriff of Alameda County, eventually led J.B. Hume to Charles E. Boles, a retired mining engineer and well-respected gentleman of San Francisco. Hume and Morse interrogated and then arrested Boles. On November 16, 1883, Boles pled guilty to the last robbery and returned the loot. He was convicted but sentenced to only six years in San Quentin Prison in return for his cooperation and good behavior. The unassuming Boles didn't drink or smoke; in fact, his worst vice was coffee.

His background was somewhat of a mystery. Born in England he came to California twice during the Gold Rush, but returned to the Midwest, married, and enlisted in the Union Army. He fought in the Civil War for three years and was seriously wounded in Georgia. Boles returned to duty as a first sergeant and was later commissioned a second lieutenant. Charles Boles was a distinguished soldier, but a lousy family man. After the war, he abandoned his wife and three daughters for the western mining country. His family had not heard from him in years and concluded that he had been killed by Indians. Charles Boles served about four years in San Quentin before being released on January 21, 1888. He was fifty-four years old. Boles disappeared after that until Detective Hume heard in 1900 that the old man had died while hunting game in the High Sierra. Black Bart may be gone, but his legend endures.

CHAPTER TWO SELECTED SOURCES

Joseph Henry Jackson, *Bad Company: The Story of California Stage-Robbers, Bandits & Highwaymen,* Harcourt Brace, New York, NY, 1949.

Jay Robert Nash, *Encyclopedia of Western Lawmen and Outlaws,* De Capo Press, New York, NY, 1989.

Ralph J. Roske, *Everyman's Eden: A History of California,* The Macmillan Company, New York, NY, 1968.

Edward B. Scott, *The Saga of Lake Tahoe, vol. I,* Sierra-Tahoe Publishing Co., Crystal Bay, Lake Tahoe, Nevada, 1957.

Stephen Goldman, *Wanted Dead or Alive: True Life Accounts of the Desperados of the Wild West,* Historical Briefs, Inc., 1994.

Lucius Beebe & Charles Clegg, *U.S. West: The Saga of Wells Fargo,* Bonanza Books, New York, NY, 1949.

Richard Dillon, *Humbugs and Heroes,* Doubleday & Company, Inc., Garden City, NY, 1970.

San Francisco *Evening Daily Bulletin,* November 14, 1883.

PHOTO CREDITS

Page 17   Corduroy mountain road, *Frank Leslie's Illustrated Newspaper,* May 24, 1879.

Page 19   Black Bart, San Francisco *Evening Daily Bulletin,* November 14, 1883.

Battle at Pyramid Lake 3

IN 1858, THE PAIUTE INDIANS of present-day northern Nevada were in the midst of a war council. The young braves were furious. White miners and settlers were encroaching on the sacred ancestral lands around Pyramid Lake, terminus of the Truckee River. The intruders were killing the game and cutting down trees from which the Indians harvested pine nuts. That very year, Indian agent Frederick Dodge had sent a report to Washington, D.C. "…the game is gone, and now, the steady tread of the white man is upon them, the green valleys too, once spotted with game are not theirs now, necessity makes them barter the virtue of their companions...Driven by destitution they seek refuge in crime."

For a time, strong leadership in the Paiute Nation kept the angry braves in check, but after the severe winter of 1859-60, the Native Americans were facing starvation. In the spring of 1860, the various tribal sects from western Nevada were calling for action against the white invaders. Old Winnemucca, leader of all the Pauites, kept his silence. The shrewd Chief was willing to let the younger men assume responsibility for this war. Chief Winnemucca was resigned to living with the white man and counseled peace. Only the brave warrior Numaga foresaw the disaster looming for his people. Numaga had little authority and he dressed in the white man's clothing, but he possessed a keen intellect and determined courage. Numaga rode from camp to camp, counseling all who would listen to seek peace with the white people. He told them, "Your enemies are like sands in the bed of the rivers; when taken away they only give place for more to come and settle." His advice was always met by a cold stony silence. One chief came to him and said, "Your skin is red, but your heart is white; go away and live among the palefaces." Suddenly, an Indian riding a foam-flecked pony dashed into the council to inform the chiefs that a group of angry braves had burned Williams' Station and killed several settlers. The bold attack occurred because the white men at the station had kidnapped two twelve-year-old Indian girls and had held them bound and gagged underneath the house. When the Indians found out, they killed the men and set fire to the house. At the news, the prescient Numaga solemnly stared in the direction of Williams' Station and said, "There is no longer any use for counsel; we must prepare for war, for the soldiers will now come here and fight us."

In Virginia City, a breathless rider stormed in from the darkness. It was James Williams, owner of the burned station. Williams had survived the attack, but his two brothers were among those killed. The horrifying news alarmed the populace. There were small isolated groups of prospectors and ranchers scattered throughout northern Nevada and the Sierra east slope. They must be protected. Excitement ran high. The savages must be punished. In the saloons that night, hundreds of young men declared their intent to ride out in the morning. Most were young and brash. Bold boasts were made over brimming beer mugs; "…an Injun for breakfast and his pony to ride." It had been a long, cold winter; the miners were restless. Panic spread quickly over the telegraph wires. But at sunrise the next day, only 105 men showed up for action. The rest had fled to California or prudently declined to join in the rash action. The military squads were a sloppy mixture of independent elements, poorly-armed, and lacking discipline and training. They still believed that the battle against the Paiute Nation would be easy, that the Indians would not fight. After all, the western Nevada tribes had generally been friendly to the whites.

The rag-tag volunteer regiments formed quickly. Captain Alanson Nightingill led the Truckee Rangers; J. Reed headed the Sierra Guards. These squads were joined by the Virginia Rifles and the Highland Rangers. John "Snowshoe" Thompson was there, mustering with the Genoa Rangers. The Carson City squad was led by Major William Ormsby, who would later die in the skirmish. Captain R. Watkins, veteran of a recent military excursion into Nicaragua where he had lost a leg, was tied to a saddle so he could once again ride into battle. Four years before, Major Ormsby and Captain Watkins had joined William Walker, who was leading a renegade army of American freebooters into Nicaragua. Walker's intent was to confiscate large tracts of Nicaraguan land and sell it to his American supporters. Although this invasive military action was not condoned by the United States government, Walker enjoyed great support back in the states. Many Americans believed in Manifest Destiny and the spread of democracy throughout the Western Hemisphere. In the duality of Manifest Destiny, conquest, profit and freedom fit hand to glove.

On May 12, 1860, the command advanced into the desert following the Truckee River. They met no resistance until they drew within two miles of the southern end of Pyramid Lake. At that point, a band of 150 Native Americans suddenly appeared on an elevated plain, just out of gunshot range. Most of the white men were armed with revolvers and shotguns, poor weapons for distance and accuracy. One volunteer who possessed a telescopic rifle was ordered to fire. The Paiutes answered with a barrage of whistling bullets. Major Ormsby told the men to tighten the girths of their saddles, they were going to war. Moments later, the major gave the order to charge. Thirty men dashed up an easy grade onto the plateau, but the Natives had disappeared. The vast landscape of sand and sagebrush seemed empty. Just then more mounted Indians were sighted, once again out of revolver or shotgun range. Slowly the men noticed that there were more warriors positioned to the east and south in a half circle. They suddenly realized that they had charged right into a trap and were now surrounded by hundreds of mounted Paiutes. More armed warriors appeared from behind the sagebrush surrounding the confused soldiers. A hail of Paiute arrows and bullets ripped through the air. The frightened horses began bucking the men, forcing them to drop their guns in order to control their mounts.

All of the men had heard stories of what happened to white men captured by Indians. The tales were chilling. Fear swept through the regiment and the men began a fast retreat to a small grove of cottonwood trees lining the Truckee River. It was a fatal mistake. The woods were swarming with warriors led by young Chiquito Winnemucca. As Chiquito and his band readied to charge the retreating soldiers, Numaga rushed between them. Unfortunately, his last attempt at a peace parley came too late; Chiquito and his braves rushed past Numaga and routed the terrified regiment. The orderly retreat became a wild, panic-stricken stampede. Where the trail narrowed and climbed a steep bank, the fleeing soldiers on horseback stalled. Chiquito and his warriors cut eight men down before the others escaped. The trail then ran out into open desert country, straight and level. The fastest horses led the retreat. The saddleless Indian ponies ran like the wind, enabling the pursuing Paiutes to take down the fleeing soldiers one by one.

During the retreat, Snowshoe Thompson's horse was shot out from under him. Snowshoe was one of the fastest men alive on skis, but now his life depended on the outcome of a foot race with the Natives. Thompson later said, "I pledge

you my word that more than once I wished that all the valley was buried in snow, and I was mounted on my snowshoes." As Thompson ran for the river, he felt hot breath over his shoulder. Expecting hand-to-hand combat with a Paiute brave, he wheeled about quickly. His elbow struck the nose of a riderless horse, saddled and bridled. He leaped onto the animal and escaped with his life. For the rest of his days, Snowshoe Thompson believed that the horse had been heaven-sent.

The Indians chased the volunteers for twenty miles, killing as many as they could. In his *History of Nevada,* Myron Angel wrote, *"Death spread over them her somber wings and silently shadowed them all."* Major Ormsby, riding an injured mule, fell to the rear. Seriously wounded, Ormsby survived until his saddle turned, throwing him to the ground. Ironically, until this rash and ill-considered battle, the major had endorsed coexistence with the Natives and was considered a friend by several of the Paiute leaders. Ormsby viewed the Paiute Nation as an ally in his fight to create a provisional territory carved out of the Mormon-dominated Utah Territory. Ormsby wanted regional sovereignty for the east slope of the Sierra and direct democracy with little or no government, principles that fed the fire of his vigilantism. But Ormsby's ambition of separatist self-determination had finally gotten the best of him. After Ormsby fell, a mounted Paiute brave approached the injured soldier of fortune. The wounded major recognized him as Natchez, the brother of Sarah Winnemucca. The compassionate Paiute told Ormsby that he would shoot high, so the wounded major could lay still and fake death. But Ormsby continued to stand, pleading, "Don't kill me, I am your friend. I'll go and talk with the whites and make peace." At that moment, Ormsby was killed by another man's bullet. His body was then rolled into the gully below.

Of the 105 white men who went into battle at Pyramid Lake, 76 were killed and several were wounded. By contrast, the Indians suffered only three warriors wounded, and two horses killed. The Paiutes later claimed that "had the battle opened two hours earlier in the day there would not have been one white survivor." They were probably right. It was only by the cover of darkness that any of the volunteers escaped.

For three days no news reached Carson and Virginia cities regarding the fate of the reckless men who had rushed out to do battle with the Natives near Pyramid Lake. Every night Indian signal fires were seen glowing on the distant ridges, but not one word from any of the missing men reached the settlements. The desert's silence was an ominous omen. Early on May 13, an exhausted rider tore into town. The man had ridden all night, nearly one hundred miles. He was covered with alkali dust and bore bad news from the battle at Pyramid Lake. There had been a massacre! The Indians had slain Major Ormsby and nearly wiped out the command. The Paiutes had trapped the soldiers like rats and killed three-fourths of them. The shocked citizens figured the man was hysterical.

Throughout the night and following morning, survivors from the battle slowly straggled in. The men told tales of horror and of a fate worse than death. One refugee claimed that he had seen thousands of mounted warriors headed for the settlements. It seemed that the Native Americans had decided to take back their country. Panic swept the Comstock and eastern Sierra. Martial law was declared in Virginia City. The town's few women and children were moved into an unfinished stone house that had been converted into a fortress called Fort Riley. Citizens organized an armed militia and picket guards were posted on the city's perimeter. At Carson City, the Penrod Hotel was barricaded with wood; and sentries were stationed around town. The residents of Silver City built a buttress of rocks where they mounted a homemade wooden cannon. Filled with scraps of iron and pieces of chain, it was meant to blast shrapnel into Indians climbing the canyon below. So many had fled over the Sierra into the safety of California, that only 106 able-bodied men were available to fight. They were doomed! Panic-stricken messages were telegraphed to cities in California — Downieville, Nevada City, and San Francisco.

News of the massacre spread like wildfire and Californians organized at once. Citizens in Sacramento and Placerville generated funds to raise militias. Downieville residents were furious to hear that Henry Meredith, a favorite local, had died in the battle. To avenge his tragic death, they recruited, armed and equipped 165 men in just thirty-six hours. This volunteer regiment, known as the Sierra Battalion, then marched from Downieville over the snow-covered Sierra to Virginia City in only five days. Miners from La Porte and farmers from Placerville also crossed the icy mountain range to join the expanding army. San Francisco sent money and arms, as well as the 6th Infantry from the Presidio and the 3rd Artillery command from Benicia. California Governor John Downey issued five hundred Minié muskets with plenty of ammunition for Nevada's defense. The Minié musket was highly accurate and lethal to a range of one-thousand yards.

In less than two weeks, hundreds of volunteers and regular troops were deployed to the Carson and Honey Lake valleys, with more arriving daily. On May 24, 1860, the Virginia Rifles marched out of Virginia City, commanded by Captain Edward Faris Storey. That same day, an army of 754 United States troops crossed the Sierra from California. When Captain Storey and the Virginia Rifles reached the Twenty-six-mile Desert, Michael Bushy was sent to scout for enemy forces along the Carson River. Bushy was a celebrated Indian fighter,

a legend from fierce battles in Oregon and Washington Territory. Unfortunately, his luck had run out and a roving band of Paiute warriors shot him dead. Bushy's bones, which were not discovered for two years, were later preserved in a box at James Small's Station near Lake Tahoe.

On May 31, at the present site of Wadsworth along the Truckee River, the Virginia Rifles were joined by the California troops equipped with howitzers and ordnance. For the next few days, the soldiers slowly made their way along the Truckee River, cautious of attack. The white men had reason to worry. In the massacre at Pyramid Lake on May 12, the Indians had possessed rifles of a longer range than the volunteers and used the desert topography to better advantage. On June 2, two feet of snow fell on the Sierra and the weather in the desert was cold and blustery. That afternoon, three hundred Paiute warriors on horseback and three hundred armed braves on foot attacked the regiments. The soldiers retreated at first, eventually regrouped, then turned to face the enemy. The Paiutes drove them back to where the desert was furrowed with rain-cut gullies, a perfect place for the Indians to make successive stands against the troops' overwhelming firepower.

The initial fight took place just two hundred yards from where Major Ormsby's body lay. Instead of one large battle, there were many separate skirmishes as the outgunned Indians slowly retreated toward their village at Pyramid Lake. On June 3, Captain Storey and twenty of his men were ordered to join Captain Van Hagen of the Nevada Rifles to take a hilltop position manned by the Paiutes. For more than three hours, there was a continuous barrage of bullets. Captain Storey led his men into the thick of the fight. They routed the Natives, killing twenty-five and capturing fifty horses. But the marginal advantage was not gained without sacrifice. Captain

Storey had fallen, mortally wounded, shot through the lungs. Captain Storey and Major Ormsby were later buried with military honors in Carson City. Storey County was named in the captain's honor.

On June 4, the American troops closed in on the Paiutes' Pyramid Lake settlement. The village was deserted. A distinct trail revealed that the Indians had fled into the Black Rock Desert. At that point, the whites declared victory and withdrew. The Paiutes are a bold and fearless tribe, but their warriors could not compete with the constant barrage from five hundred rapid-load Minié muskets in the hands of trained, determined soldiers. In fact, it is amazing that in the second battle, the warriors were able to advance on the regiments for five hours before being turned back. No one knows for certain how many Paiutes were killed. The Indians claimed only four dead and seven wounded; other casualty estimates ranged from 46 to 160. Regardless, the toll from the Pyramid Lake War was tragic for both sides. An uneasy peace was secured; Fort Churchill was built on the Carson River, and Indian reservations were established at Pyramid and Walker lakes. The white man was here to stay, and the Paiutes' way of life would never be the same.

CHAPTER THREE SELECTED SOURCES

Chris W. Bayer, *Profit, Plots and Lynching—Mormon Station, the founding of Carson City and the creation of Nevada Territory,* a Neato Stuff publication, Carson City, Nevada, 1995.

Guy Louis Rocha, *Nevada's Emergence in the American Great Basin,* Nevada Historical Society Quarterly, Winter 1995.

Hubert Howe Bancroft, *History of Nevada, Colorado, and Wyoming 1540 – 1888,* Volume XXV, The History Company, San Francisco, California, 1890.

Myron Angel, *History of San Luis Obispo County California,* Thompson & West, Oakland, California, 1883.

Thomas Wren, *A History of the State of Nevada; Its Resources and People,* The Lewis Publishing Company, New York, NY, 1904.

William C. Miller, *The Pyramid Lake Indian War of 1860, Parts One & Two,* Nevada Historical Society Quarterly, September & November, 1957.

Henry De Groot, & J. Wells Kelly, *First Directory of Nevada Territory,* Valentine & Company, San Francisco, California, 1862.

Myron Angel, *History of Nevada,* Thompson & West, Oakland, California, 1881.

Samuel G. Houghton, *A Trace of Desert Waters,* University of Nevada Press, Reno, Nevada, 1994.

John M. Townley, *The Pyramid Lake Indian War,* Desert Rat Guidebook Series.

Dan De Quille (William Wright), *The Big Bonanza,* Alfred A. Knopf, New York, NY, 1947.

Richard A. Dwyer and Richard E. Lingenfelter, *Dan De Quille, The Washoe Giant,* University of Nevada Press, Reno and Las Vegas, Nevada, 1990.

George D. Lyman, *The Saga of the Comstock Lode,* Charles Scribner's Sons, New York, 1934.

Virginia City *Territorial Enterprise,* June 21, 1872.

San Francisco Chronicle, July 11, 1878.

Sacramento Union, May 14, 15, 19, 1860.

Nevada State Journal, July 11, 1878.

PHOTO CREDITS

| Page 27 | Indian Attack! London *Graphic,* August 26, 1876, by John S. Davis. |
| Page 31 | Soldier dragged by horse, *Harper's Weekly,* June 8, 1889, by Frederic Remington. |

Nancy Kelsey: First White Woman Over the Sierra

Much has been written of the Donner Party's tragic entrapment in the deep Sierra snow during the winter of 1846-47. Those with a cursory knowledge of America's 19th century westward migration are also familiar with the Stephens Party, which successfully crossed Truckee's Pass in 1844 and opened the California Trail. But fewer are aware of the Bidwell-Bartleson Party, a group of thirty-four plucky pioneers who survived a trans-Sierra crossing in 1841. They were the first organized group of American emigrants to reach California via the overland trail. Although the Bidwell-Bartleson Party failed to bring their wagons all the way to California, their epic journey proved that a direct crossing to the Pacific Ocean was indeed feasible.

In the late 1830s, overland emigration to Oregon was well-established, but the route to California was still unknown. For most Americans in 1841, it was much easier and faster to reach Europe than California. Nothing was known of present-day northern Utah and Nevada except what trappers had reported. The only parties known to have crossed this harsh desert country were two groups of mountain men led by the famed frontiersmen Jedediah Smith and Joseph Walker.

These bands of early American trappers and explorers had traversed Nevada via the Ogden River, later re-named the Humboldt, which flows east to west across the region. There were also a few men who had made it overland to California traveling the Old Spanish Trail from Santa Fe. Among them were French trapper Antoine Robidoux and Harvard-educated, pseudo-physician, John Marsh. Robidoux later returned to Missouri, where he gave lectures extolling the health and virtues of California's mild climate and pastoral landscape. Midwest newspapers published numerous letters Marsh had sent from his ranch near Mount Diablo in the Sacramento Valley, proclaiming the unlimited opportunities on the Pacific Coast.

Lured by the tales of optimism, adventurous pioneers in the frontier states along the Mississippi River formed the Western Emigration Society. Hundreds of Midwesterners signed a contract to meet in May 1841 at Sapling Grove, outside of Independence, Missouri. There on the banks of the Missouri River, they would organize the first California-bound wagon train. It seemed that all of western Missouri was gearing up for a mass exodus. Merchants and business owners panicked that the region would become a veritable ghost town. Editorials ridiculing the risky venture were published in the local press. Thomas Farnham, who had an unfortunate experience with Mexican authorities in 1839, wrote about the possibility of cruel treatment to foreigners in California. The negative campaign scared off all but the boldest pioneers.

On May 1, only John Bidwell, a twenty-one-year-old school teacher, his companion George Henshaw, and one other wagon with several people showed up for the trek west to California. Although the Oregon Trail was fairly well established in 1841, the undiscovered California trail was an unmapped trek into a trackless wilderness. Eventually sixty-nine pioneers gathered at Sapling Grove for the overland journey, but only half of them were headed for Marsh's ranch in California. In the Oregon-bound group was a Jesuit priest, Pierre Jean De Smet, who was accompanied by other Jesuit priests and lay brothers. The Jesuits were heading west to convert the Indians of the Flathead Nation. Shortly after striking out for the plains on May 10, eight men on horseback led by John Bartleson, overtook the slow, creaking wagons. Bartleson claimed to have a letter from John Marsh, in which Marsh described a direct route to the Sacramento Valley. Since Bartleson held the letter, he demanded command of the group. Despite misgivings that he possessed limited leadership qualities, Bartleson was elected captain, with the popular John Bidwell voted in as secretary. Bidwell, leading spirit of the party and later one of the most prominent men on the Pacific Coast, wrote, "Bartleson was not the best man for the position, but we were given to understand that if he was not elected captain, he would not go; he had seven or eight men with him and we did not want the party diminished."

Among the emigrants was the large Kelsey family from Kentucky. Most of the Kelsey family was bound for Oregon, a few for California. Only two brothers, Andrew and Benjamin, with Benjamin's eighteen-year-old wife, Nancy and her infant daughter Martha Ann in tow, chose the latter destination. The daughter of hearty pioneers, Nancy was born in Barren County, Kentucky, on August 1, 1823. Three years later the family moved to Missouri. When Nancy turned sixteen she married Benjamin Kelsey. Less than two years later, the young couple picked up and left for California. Excluding Nancy and six-month-old Martha Ann, the Bidwell-Bartleson Party consisted of unmarried young men seeking adventure. One thing they all had in common was their ignorance of frontier skills and Indian lore. Only half had some knowledge of firearms, and fewer still were accomplished hunters. The little experience that they had with wagons and livestock came from farming. Their crude, wooden vehicles varied from two-wheeled carts to overloaded farm wagons. They brought some cured meats, but it was assumed that hunters would provide fresh game along the way.

Unfortunately, their maps were worthless. So complete was their ignorance of the geography of the arid Great Basin, that the pioneers took tools along for the purpose of building canoes. They intended to sail from the Great Salt Lake to the Pacific Ocean. In their journey west, the emigrants followed a virtual highway of rivers. In May they crossed the Missouri, and followed the Kansas to the Little Blue River into present-day Kansas. After a close call with a band of well-armed Cheyenne Indians, they successfully traversed the treacherous South Fork of the Platte River, reaching Fort Laramie on June 22. They had traveled 625 miles in forty-two days, an average of fifteen miles per day. But there were more dangers than hostile Indians, poisonous snakes, and rushing rivers. Near Fort Laramie they were nearly killed by severe weather. In his diary, John Bidwell wrote, "First came a terrific shower, followed by a fall of hail to the depth of four inches, some of the stones being as large as turkey eggs; and the next day a waterspout — an angry, huge, whirling cloud column which seemed to draw its water from the Platte River — passed within a quarter of a mile behind us…Had it struck us, it doubtless would have demolished us."

In early August the Bidwell-Bartleson Party split from the other pioneers heading for Oregon country. Back in Missouri, Father De Smet had hired an experienced mountain man, Thomas "Broken Hand" Fitzpatrick, to pilot their wagons to Fort Hall. His leadership and knowledge of the wilderness had gotten them this far. One of the Jesuit priests wrote, "In these immense solitudes it was necessary to have an experienced guide. The choice fell not on the colonel (Bartleson), who had never crossed the mountains, but on the captain Father De Smet had engaged. He was a courageous Irishman,

known to most of the Indian tribes as Broken Hand. He had spent fully two thirds of his life crossing the plains." Old Broken Hand, who had saved the wagon train in their encounter with the Cheyenne Indians, pleaded with the young greenhorns to stay on the Oregon Trail. Captain Fitzpatrick's words of prudence bore fruit. Twelve of the California-bound took the grizzled guide's sage advice, but thirty-two men, plus Nancy Kelsey and her baby, were still determined to reach California. When other members of the Kelsey family asked Nancy why she would risk her baby's life on the untested California trail, she replied, "Where my husband goes, I go. I can better endure the hardships of the journey, than the anxieties for an absent husband."

Many tears were shed by the close knit pioneers when the small wagon train split into two at the trail's fork to Oregon. It was likely that neither group would see the other again. Desperate for fresh provisions and hopeful for information about what lay ahead, Captain Bartleson took three men and rode on for another forty miles to Fort Hall in order to hire a guide and purchase more supplies. This splinter group would later rendezvous with the main wagon train near the only recognizable landmark they knew of, the Great Salt Lake. No one in the party possessed accurate information about California or how to get there. In his letters, Marsh had reported the latitude of San Francisco Bay. The pioneers could only compare that with the latitude of their starting point in Independence, Missouri. Their maps were worthless. Bidwell later wrote, "Our ignorance of the route was complete. We knew that California lay west and that was the extent of our knowledge. Our maps showed a lake in the vicinity of where Salt Lake now is; but it was represented as a long lake, three or four hundred miles in extent, narrow and with two outlets, both running into the Pacific Ocean, either apparently larger than the Mississippi River."

The famed explorer Jedediah Smith had already disproved the existence of the mythical River San Buenaventura, but older maps still included this non-existent waterway connecting the Great Salt Lake and San Francisco Bay. For the Bidwell-Bartleson Party, their anticipated easy canoe ride to the Pacific Ocean had turned into a long march through desiccated salt flats and the dry, alkali dust of the desert. Not only had their outdated map placed a major river where one did not exist, it also failed to include the immense wall of the Sierra Nevada.

Near Fort Hall on the Snake River, the brave pioneers veered off the Oregon Trail and turned south. The four men who had continued on to Fort Hall inquired about a possible California trail. The commander of the outpost, Captain Grant, informed them there was no guide available to go with them. But he did tell them that it was critical to find the Humboldt River: "You must strike out west of Salt Lake...being careful not to go too far south, lest you get into a waterless country without grass. You must be careful not to go by way of the canyons as trapping parties have done and become bewildered and perish." Captain Grant's valuable advice was shared with Bidwell and the others when the volunteers rejoined the main party. The ragged group traveled around the north end of Salt Lake into the waterless, salt-encrusted desert. They wandered for days, choked by alkali dust and burned by the desert sun. They suffered from extreme thirst and their meager provisions were already running low. Joseph Chiles, a member of the party and future leader of other emigrant wagon trains, later stated that they traveled seven months with no guide, no compass, and nothing but the sun to direct them west.

Despite the seriousness of their situation, the spirit of the restless young men could not be stifled. One hot day, Jimmy John challenged John Bidwell to a race to reach the top of a snow-capped mountain nearby. Distances are deceptive in the arid West, and darkness overtook the two adventurers before they reached the snowline. Flickering fires on the desert floor far below indicated possibly hostile Indians, so the boys were forced to spend a cold night on the mountainside without food or blankets. Dawn found them huddled for warmth with the snowfield tantalizingly close. The stubborn duo refused to give up, and they continued to climb for the snow. They achieved their frosty goal mid-morning, filled a neckerchief with snow, and then high-tailed it back to the wagon train. Somehow Bidwell and Jimmy John managed to elude the vigilant Indian sentinels. They finally rejoined their friends in the westbound wagons and carts, who had sadly given them up for dead. Captain Bartleson loudly reprimanded the two for risking their lives for a snowball, but happily, the party was once again intact.

August arrived and the hot sun scorched the desert sand, but at night the temperature was so cold ice formed in their water buckets. The weather was extreme and the landscape seemed devoid of life.

Their luck held and two weeks later they stumbled upon the south fork of the Humboldt River. They were only the third party to cross the Rockies and bring wagons into what is now Nevada. However, by September 15, it became evident that they must travel faster if they were to beat the Sierra's deadly winter snowstorms. They abandoned their wagons and rigged saddle-packs for their mules, horses, and oxen. It wasn't easy. None of them had ever packed animals before. The stubborn mules bucked and kicked at the bulky packs, and the hungry oxen jumped and bellowed, trying to throw off their heavy loads. That night they cooked their supper with fires made from the discarded wagons. As they sat down to eat their meager food, a Shoshone Indian appeared. The sage Native American said that the Great Spirit had told him that he would find a strange people here who would give him many things. He was right. The emigrants did give him many of their abandoned possessions, the first being a pair of pants for his naked body.

As the emigrants struggled west along the Humboldt River, they were forced to kill their emaciated oxen for food. When they ran out of tobacco, they cut out their old pockets and chewed on them. They were a pitiful sight. The men shuffled silently through the desert dust. There was no energy for boisterous shenanigans now. Nancy Kelsey was carrying little Martha Ann in her arms, walking barefoot, and leading her horse. In early October, Captain Bartleson and his eight men killed one of the remaining oxen, took a double share of the meat, and rode off on horses. Bartleson shouted back to the others, "If you can keep up with us, all right; if you cannot, you may go to hell! We are going to California." One of his men would not go with the irresponsible captain. He said, "The captain is wrong, and I will stay with you boys." Those in charge of the slow-moving oxen could not keep up with the men on horseback and were forced to follow Bartleson's faint trail. They lost it in windswept sand south of the Humboldt Sink. By following Bartleson south, the emigrants missed the luxuriant Truckee Meadows just a short distance to the west. It wasn't until Chief Truckee revealed the verdant meadows to Elisha Stephens in 1844 that California-bound pioneers were able to take advantage of the abundant water and nutritious grass growing there.

The main party was split on whether to continue west or return to the safety of Fort Hall. A vote was held and the majority wanted to keep going for California. At that point, John Bidwell, and Nancy's husband, Benjamin Kelsey, took charge of the ragged group. They crossed the Carson River heading south. They reached the Walker River, which they mistook for the San Joaquin. Marsh had described the San Joaquin River as the main route up California's Central Valley. The faltering emigrants soon realized their mistake as they struggled west, up the steep Walker River Canyon. Their total food supply consisted of some dried meat and two emaciated oxen.

As they climbed the rough canyon up into the rugged Sierra, Captain Bartleson and his followers who had abandoned the main group nine days before rode into camp. They had gone too far south and gotten lost in the desert. Exhausted and starving, they were also suffering from dysentery brought on by the pine nuts and fish fed them by the Walker Lake Indians. The Bidwell–Kelsey group held no grudge against Bartleson and his men, so they fed the crestfallen men from their meager supply of provisions. Refreshed by the food and water, but humbled by his recent experience, Captain Bartleson exclaimed, "Boys! My hogs in Missouri fared better than I have of late, and if ever I see that spot again I swear to you I will never leave that country." Although the once portly captain seemed to be a changed man, he later abandoned the party again.

The emigrants had eaten the last of the oxen and were now killing their horses and mules for food. While crossing the precipitous Sierra, several of the pack animals lost their footing on the granite cliffs and fell to their deaths. Yet the desperate little band pressed on. Finally, on October 18, they crossed the Pacific Divide and descended down the Stanislaus River Canyon and into the San Joaquin Valley. The valley was brown from drought, but the starving pioneers saw only the numerous herds of grazing elk. They arrived at Dr. Marsh's ranch on November 4, 1841. The Bidwell-Bartleson Party's successful overland crossing into California inspired other emigrants to roll their wagons west. No lives were lost in the 1841 crossing, and Nancy Kelsey and her daughter Martha Ann, the first American women to cross the Sierra Nevada, proved that women could stand the arduous journey.

Nancy Kelsey's adventures did not end upon her arrival in California. In fact, they were just beginning. Nancy and Benjamin briefly settled in Napa Valley before traveling overland to Oregon in 1843. They returned to Napa Valley in 1844, driving a large herd of cattle in order to start up a ranch. Both trips to and from Oregon were plagued by hostile Indians. In 1845, a second daughter, Mary, was born at Sutter's Fort. Her third daughter, Nancy, was born in 1851. Nancy Kelsey witnessed the Bear Flag Rebellion and the capture of Sonoma in 1846. She provided the cloth and helped sew the original California Bear Flag. In 1848, Nancy's husband Benjamin joined in the Gold Rush. At the Kelsey's Diggings in present-day El Dorado County, he shoveled out $10,000 worth of gold in just two days. In addition, he supplied the other miners with sheep, netting $16,000 in one deal alone. After all their effort and hardship, California had treated the Kelsey family well.

Nancy died in 1896 and was buried in the Cuyama Mountains in Southern California.

In an interview before she died, she pronounced her own epitaph: *"I have enjoyed riches and suffered the pangs of poverty. I have seen U.S. Grant when he was little known. I have baked bread for Fremont and talked with Kit Carson. I have run from bear and killed most other smaller game...you will have to be satisfied with that for the present."*

CHAPTER ONE SELECTED SOURCES

Dr. Doyce B. Nunis, Jr., *The Bidwell-Bartleson Party: 1841 California Emigrant Adventure,* Western Tanager Press, Santa Cruz, California, 1991.

Leroy R. Hafen, *Broken Hand: The Life of Thomas Fitzpatrick, Mountain Man, Guide and Indian Agent*, University of Nebraska Press, Lincoln, Nebraska, 1973.

John D. Unruh, Jr., *The Plains Across: The Overland Emigrants and the Trans-Mississippi West, 1840 – 1860*, University of Illinois Press, Chicago, Illinois, 1993.

Rockwell D. Hunt, *John Bidwell: Prince of California Pioneers,* The Caxton Printers, Ltd., Caldwell, Idaho, 1942.

Joanne McCubrey, *The First Pioneer Woman to Cross the Sierra,* article *Sierra Heritage Magazine,* Auburn, California, Nov.-Dec. 1991.

Robert Glass Cleland, *Pathfinders,* Powell Publishing Company, Los Angeles, California, 1929.

James G. Scrugham, *Nevada – A Narrative of the Conquest of a*

Frontier Land, Vol. I, The American Historical Society, Inc., Chicago & New York, 1935.

Ray Allen Billington, *The Far Western Frontier 1830 – 1860,* University of New Mexico Press, Albuquerque, New Mexico, 1956.

Philip Ault, *Pioneer Nancy Kelsey, Californians Magazine,* March/April, 1992.

Hubert Howe Bancroft, *History of California, vol. I – IV* and *History of Nevada, Colorado, Wyoming 1540 – 1888, vol.XXV,* The History Company, San Francisco, California, 1886 & 1890.

John Bidwell, *Echoes of the Past, Century Illustrated Monthly Magazine,* 1890 – 91.

Donovan Lewis, *Pioneers of California: True Stories of Early Settlers in the Golden State,* Scottwall Associates, San Francisco, California, 1993.

Twain on Tahoe 5

A CLASSIC IMAGE from nineteenth century San Francisco or Virginia City is famed writer and humorist Mark Twain, poised with his favorite cigar. He was a small man, weighing less than one hundred fifty pounds, with dark brown hair and a bushy red mustache. His wit was legend and his love of cigars obsessive. Twain's story of success was planted on the Comstock — it blossomed in San Francisco.

Samuel Clemens lurched stiffly out of the cramped stage-coach and squinted into the bright desert sun. It was August 14, 1861. Twenty-five-year-old Clemens and his older brother, Orion, had just traveled nearly two thousand miles — twenty days of rough road and alkali dust — stuffed into the Spartan interior of a Concord stagecoach. After what seemed like an eternity, the two young men had finally arrived in Carson City, capital of Nevada Territory, so that Orion could assume his duties as the newly appointed territorial secretary. Overland stage passengers were permitted only twenty-five pounds of luggage per person. To cut weight, Samuel and Orion were forced to leave most of their personal belongings behind. Their bare essentials for survival, however, included five pounds of tobacco.

Exhausted and thirsty, the brothers slapped the dust from their clothes and strolled toward the nearest saloon. Clemens later described early Carson City as "…a wooden town; its population two thousand souls. The main street consisted of four or five blocks of little white frame stores which were too high to sit down on, but not too high for various other purposes; in fact, hardly high enough. The houses are unplastered, but papered inside with flour sacks sewed together—and the handsomer the brand upon the sacks, the neater the house looks. The [houses] were packed together, side by side, as if room was scarce in that mighty plain." Born and raised in Missouri, Clemens was shocked by the barrenness of the Great Basin. Shortly after his arrival, Sam wrote his mother back East; "It never rains here, and the dew never falls. No flowers grow here, and no green thing gladdens the eye. The birds that fly over the land carry their provisions with them. Only the crow and the raven tarry with us."

At first, Clemens wasn't impressed with the western landscape, but a short trip to beautiful Lake Tahoe quickly changed his mind. Samuel Clemens had heard of the majestic pine forests surrounding Lake Tahoe, so he and John Kinney, a young man from Cincinnati, decided to stake a timber claim along the north shore of the great lake. They packed their supplies over the Carson Range and down into the Tahoe Basin. Their first glimpse of the lake overwhelmed them. Clemens described Lake Tahoe as "a noble sheet of blue water lifted six thousand three hundred feet above the level of the seas, and walled in by a rim of snow-clad mountain peaks that towered aloft a full three thousand feet higher still! It is a vast oval, and one would have to use up eighty or a hundred good miles in traveling around it. As it lay there with the shadows of the mountains brilliantly photographed upon its still surface, I thought it must surely be the fairest picture the whole world affords."

After supper that night, the boys broke out their pipes. It was a glorious experience; "As the darkness closed down and the stars came out and spangled the great mirrors with jewels, we smoked meditatively in the solemn hush and forgot our troubles and pains." But the mellow experience was lost when the two tenderfoots accidentally started a fire which burned down part of the forest. Later Sam had to apologize to authorities in Carson City. He was forgiven after payment of damages. Sam had not forgotten his family back in Missouri. He staked a Tahoe timber claim for his sister, Pamela, and her husband, William Moffett, on what he immodestly called "Sam Clemens Bay." He found the area so beautiful that he wrote, "I'll build a county seat there one of these days that will make the Devil's mouth water if he ever visits the earth." But cutting timber proved too strenuous for the two young men and they soon returned to Carson City. In the decades ahead, Clemens, known later of course as Mark Twain—would travel the world, visiting its most famous sights, but he always considered Tahoe the most beautiful lake of all, the "masterpiece of the universe."

It wasn't long before the Clemens brothers were hard bitten by gold fever. Stories of instant wealth were told over beer every night in the saloons. Freight wagons laden with rich ore, sometimes garnished with bricks of pure gold and silver, constantly rumbled down the Commercial Row in Carson City. The brothers were soon speculating, purchasing "feet" in various claims around the region. Most of the mining claims, however, were worthless. Sam spent months tramping around the desert, searching for his own El Dorado. These were difficult times for the man who would later become one of America's most celebrated writers. Samuel Clemens had been a prestigious and well-paid Mississippi River pilot before he came west. Now his money was gone and it seemed that his chance to strike it rich had eluded him. In his book *Roughing It,* Twain complains, "We were stark mad with excitement...drunk with happiness...smothered under mountains of prospective wealth...arrogantly compassionate toward the plodding millions who knew not our marvelous canyon…but our credit was not good at the grocer's." Twain claimed that, "A mine is a hole in the ground, owned by a liar."

Clemens' sister, Pamela, wrote him that he could always return to piloting on the Mississippi. Mining was tough, but Sam was not returning to the river. He told her, "What in thunder are pilot's wages to me?…I never have once thought of returning home to go on the river again, and I never expect to do any more piloting at any price. My livelihood must be made in this country." Sam Clemens should have been wielding a quill pen, not a miner's pick. But things were about to change. Cooped up in his cabin at Aurora during the spring thaw of 1862, Clemens wrote several burlesque sketches for the *Territorial Enterprise* newspaper in Virginia City. They were short, humorous stories about hard-luck miners, which Sam penned under the pseudonym "Josh." The sketches were funny and fit perfectly with the tone of humor found on the Comstock. The *Territorial Enterprise* liked the articles and hired the unknown writer. First started when W.L. Jernegan and Alfred James hired John "Snowshoe" Thompson to carry a small printing press over the Sierra from California, the *Enterprise* began as a weekly in Genoa, Nevada, on December 18, 1858. The *Territorial Enterprise* and its office were relocated to Carson City the following year. New owners then moved the paper to Virginia City in November 1860, where it became a morning daily.

The paper's printing press and compositor's quarters were situated in a small, one-story frame building with a lean-to on one side. Twenty-four-year-old Joseph Goodman was the editor-in-chief. Self-educated but loaded with talent, Goodman had a knack for hiring gifted writers. He and Mark Twain would become lifelong friends. Goodman managed his staff journalists with a free hand, but he demanded that their

stories be entertaining and based on fact. At first, Sam Clemens wasn't ready to completely give up his mining career for writing. But after another fruitless summer in 1862, he limped into Virginia City in early September. He had been walking for about a week when he stumbled into the office of the *Enterprise*. He collapsed into a chair and gasped, "My starboard leg seems to be unshipped. I'd like about one hundred yards of line; I think I am falling to pieces. My name is Clemens and I've come to write for the paper." The former river pilot *cum* newspaperman had docked in the desert.

Sam teamed up with another young staff reporter, William Wright, better known as Dan De Quille. De Quille penned serious political and mining news, but his real talent lay in writing ironic sketches and humorous hoaxes. De Quille was the perfect colleague for Clemens and they became friends and roommates. Clemens quickly became the most popular writer on the Comstock. When questioned as to his writing style, he later stated, "The difference between the almost right word and the right word is really a large matter—'tis the difference between the lightning-bug and the lightning." While the *Enterprise* staff worked, they smoked cigars, drank beer and ate Limburger cheese, a popular combination among newsmen. Clemens had smoked since he was a boy and now had a cigar or pipe in his mouth every waking hour. Twain stated that " He never smoked when asleep and never refrained when awake." Years later he reminisced, "when they used to tell me I would shorten my life ten years by smoking…they little knew how trivial and valueless I would regard a decade that had no smoking in it."

After all those months in the crude mining camps, Clemens was ready to revel in the excitement of Virginia City. He had a roof over his head, fifteen restaurants to eat at, and fifty-one saloons to drink in. Nearly everyday a gunfight or robbery made headlines. It is said that the first twenty-six graves in the Virginia City cemetery are occupied by murdered men. Occasionally, the wild frontier town was quiet and Clemens would get desperate for news. During one of these lulls, word reached the *Enterprise* staff that a desperado had killed a man in a saloon. In the newspaper story, Sam thanked the desperado with typical droll humor: "Sir, you are a stranger to me, but you have done me a kindness this day which I can never forget. If whole years of gratitude can be any slight compensation, they shall be yours. I was in trouble and you have relieved me nobly and at a time when all seemed dark and drear. Count me your friend from this time forth, for I am not a man to forget a favor."

More often than not, however, there was plenty of action to be found along the dusty streets of Virginia City. The townsfolk consisted of Irish, English, German, Native American and Chinese miners, gamblers and toughs. The principle industries were hard-rock mining, boisterous saloons and prostitution. The colorful excitement and wild recklessness suited Sam fine. His years as a riverboat pilot had toughened him and the Comstock's robust lifestyle fed his spirit.

During the winter of 1863, Goodwin assigned Sam to cover the territory's constitutional convention and other legislative events in Carson City. Clemens was bored in Carson City. He wrote, "The legislature sat sixty days and passed private toll-road franchises all the time. When they adjourned it was estimated that every citizen owned about three franchises, and it was believed that unless Congress gave the Territory another degree of longitude there would not be room enough to accommodate the toll-roads." In was in February 1863 that Samuel Clemens first signed an article, "Mark Twain," a name that would become world famous. Mark Twain is a nautical term used by sailors for a water depth of two fathoms, or twelve feet deep. Other accounts claim that once Clemens got his job, he was able to obtain credit at the saloons. Ordering two drinks was customary so Sam would tell the bartender to mark "twain" on the credit chalkboard. One witness later said "Clemens was by no means a Coal Oil Tommy, he drank for the pure and unadulterated love of the ardent...his parting injunction was to "mark twain" meaning two chalk marks...in this way...he acquired the title which has since become famous."

In addition to the saloons, Virginia City sported a fine opera house that attracted world class performers. During the theater season of 1863-64, Adah Isaacs Menken visited the Comstock after her long tour at Tom Maquire's Opera House in San Francisco. She had performed for sixty nights there, at $500 per night. Her role as a sensuous Lady Godiva, in which she wore a body stocking that made her look naked, had captured the heart of San Francisco. Now she was coming to Washoe. Adah Menken was a 19th century poet and stage performer who had gained international fame for her artistic talent and scandalous, tempestuous love affairs. Among her many ex-husbands was, John C. Hennan, a.k.a. "Benicia Boy," a world famous prizefighter from Benicia, California. Her debut in Virginia City packed the house; every seat was sold out. The miners had been dreaming of "La Menken" ever since her arrival in California. Twain also worked as stage critic for the *Enterprise* and had attended one of her performances in San Francisco. Like the rest of the audience, he fell under her spell and wrote a laudatory critique for the paper. Menken's spell didn't last forever because several years later Mark Twain wrote to the San Francisco *Alta California* newspaper criticizing her for using and abandoning famous people. He also complained that "She has beautiful white hands, but her handwriting is infamous; she writes fast, and her calligraphy is of the doorplate order—her letters are immense."

The end of Mark Twain's career in Nevada came suddenly. The Civil War was raging back East and emotions on the Comstock were running hot. In May 1864, *Territorial Enterprise* editor Joe Goodman was away from Virginia City and Mark Twain was acting as editor. Twain's ego had grown mightily since his miserable mining days and now that the boss was gone it was time to stir the pot. Twain accused the staff of the rival *Virginia Daily Union* newspaper of failing to honor their pledge in donating money to the Sanitary Commission. Money collected by the Commission was earmarked for medical supplies for wounded Union soldiers fighting in the Civil War. In retaliation to that accusation, James Laird, editor of the *Union,* called Twain a "vulgar liar." In an editorial response in the *Enterprise,* Mark Twain retorted, "I denounce Laird as an unmitigated liar." Twain then sent a personal note to Laird; "If you do not wish yourself posted as a coward, you will at once accept my peremptory challenge."

Suddenly the newsprint warfare had escalated into the challenge of a duel, with loaded pistols, not empty words. Reacting to the spat under the heading, "The Duello in Virginia," the editor of the San Francisco *Morning Call* wrote, "It is well, perhaps, that only ink instead of blood has been shed in this affair, but it would have appeared better if neither had been spilt. The day has gone by when duels can give any man credit for bravery or honor, wisdom or truth." In the meantime, Mark Twain's unfettered pen had also stirred the ire of Carson City's women society. Twain alleged that the money the women had raised for the wounded Union soldiers was instead being sent to the St. Louis Exposition. The women were furious at his irresponsible remarks and called them a "tissue of falsehoods, made for malicious purposes." Mark Twain was now in serious trouble in both Virginia and Carson cities. Although exciting stories of a gunfight between Twain and his editorial adversary on the *Virginia City Union* still persist today, in reality, the Laird-Twain duel never materialized. Nevada had recently passed a law making it a felony to send or accept a challenge to a duel. Threatened with a possible arrest, Mark Twain quietly stole away from the diminishing excitement on the economically depressed Comstock. Accompanied by his friend, Steve Gillis, they arrived in San Francisco in late May.

With a population over 130,000 people, cosmopolitan San Francisco had numerous daily newspapers, opera houses, fine hotels, restaurants and other amenities. Mark Twain fell in love with the city by the bay. Gillis took a job on the San Francisco *Morning Call* as a compositor. Mark joined the staff as a reporter. The spirited young men roomed together and made the most of the city, drinking, smoking, and playing billiards, Twain's favorite game. Mark enjoyed riding the horse-drawn omnibus to the Ocean House at Seal Point. At the Ocean House he dined on fried Eastern oysters, quenched his thirst at the bar and gazed at the sea lions through binoculars. Young and reckless, Twain and Gillis changed hotels seven times in the first four months. Although Mark Twain was readily accepted by San Francisco's literary community, he was dissatisfied with his position on the *Morning Call*. In Virginia City, Mark had been able to write about anything he wanted. As just another staff reporter on the *Morning Call,* however, he felt cramped. Everything he wrote seemed in conflict with the paper's policies or politics. He later wrote, "It was fearful drudgery—soulless drudgery—and almost destitute of interest. It was awful slavery for a lazy man, and I was born lazy."

Mark Twain spent two years in California where he became famous for the publication of his "Jumping Frog Story." But Twain's days in San Francisco were coming to an end. Mark Twain sailed for the Sandwich Islands in March 1866. He would soon become an established literary figure and celebrity lecturer. Mark Twain returned to Nevada in November 1866. Thousands came to hear his lectures at Dayton, Virginia City, Gold Hill, and Carson City. Journalist Alfred Doten described Mark Twain's speaking style; "Twain combined the most valuable of statistical and general information, with passages of the drollest humor—all delivered in the peculiar and inimitable style of the author—and rising occasionally to lofty flights and descriptive eloquence."

After his last lecture at Gold Hill, Mark and his agent, Dennis McCarthy, walked back to Virginia City. On the way, they were robbed by five highwaymen. The bandits took $125 in coin and Mark's favorite gold watch which was worth about $300. Twain was livid. Nevertheless, he put an advertisement in the morning paper offering to negotiate for the watch. He received no response. Two days later Mark Twain had boarded the Pioneer Stage for his return to San Francisco via the Donner Lake route. Just as the stage was about to leave, a small package was handed to the sullen celebrity. In it he found his watch and money that had been stolen from him. He also discovered the five masks that the "highwaymen" had worn that night. And then the robbers themselves revealed their identities by shaking Twain's hand. They were old friends from the Virginia City days, but Mark Twain, the prankster, could not take the joke, and everyone could hear him yelling profanities as the stagecoach rolled out of sight. Such was Mark Twain's exit from the Silver State.

When Mark Twain was born on November 30, 1835, Halley's Comet was ablaze in the evening sky. Halley's is a

famous periodic comet with a 75-year return cycle. Throughout his life, Mark Twain predicted that he would "go out with
the comet." He spent decades working on a book portraying
the comet as his cosmic counterpart. Mark Twain died quietly at his home in Connecticut on April 21, 1910. That night,
Halley's Comet was high overhead, burning bright.

CHAPTER FOUR SELECTED SOURCES

R. Kent Rasmussen, *Mark Twain A to Z – The Essential Reference to His Life and Writings,* Facts on File Incorporated, New York, NY, 1995.

George J. Williams III, *On the Road with Mark Twain in California and Nevada,* Tree By The River Publishing, Dayton, Nevada, 1994.

Mark Twain, *Roughing It,* Harper & Brothers Publishers, New York, NY, 1871.

Katherine Hillyer, *Young Reporter Mark Twain in Virginia City,* Western Printing and Publishing Company, Sparks, Nevada, 1964.

Guy Cardwell, *The Man Who Was Mark Twain,* Yale University Press, New Haven, CT, 1991.

Mark Twain, *Mark Twain's Own Autobiography,* reprint with introduction and notes by Michael J. Kiskis, The University of Wisconsin Press, Madison, Wisconsin, 1990.

Bruce Michelson, *Mark Twain on the Loose,* University of Massachusetts Press, Amherst, Massachusetts, 1995.

Ivan Benson, *Mark Twain's Western Years,* Stanford University Press, Stanford University, California, 1938.

Margaret Sanborn, *Mark Twain: The Bachelor Years,* Doubleday Publishing, New York, NY, 1990.

Journals of Alfred Doten 1849 – 1903, edited by Walter Van Tilburg Clark, University of Nevada Press, Reno, Nevada, 1973.

Chris W. Bayer, *Profit, Plots and Lynching – Mormon Station, the founding of Carson City and the creation of Nevada Territory,* a Neato Stuff publication, Carson City, Nevada, 1995.

Paul Fatout, *Mark Twain in Virginia City,* Indiana University Press, 1964.

Effie Mona Mack, *Mark Twain in Nevada,* Charles Scribner's Sons, London, England, 1947.

William R. Gillis, *Gold Rush Days with Mark Twain,* Albert & Charles Boni Publishing, New York, NY, 1930.

San Francisco Chronicle, March 30, 1919,

PHOTO CREDITS

Page 55   Mark Twain, *Courtesy of Sylvia Stoddard,* Carson City, Nevada.

Page 61   Advertisement for Virginia City *Territorial Enterprise,* 1862.

Alice Hartley: The Madness of Meadow Lake

FOR MORE THAN HALF A CENTURY, from 1899 to 1951, students in the Tahoe-Truckee school districts attended classes at Truckee's Meadow Lake Union High School. Surprisingly, despite the popularity and proximity of both Lake Tahoe and Donner Lake, the school was named after a small, shallow alpine lake, located miles away on the west slope of the Sierra Nevada. Obscure Meadow Lake may lack name recognition, but it looms large in the annals of Sierra history.

Located at 7,254 feet between the headwaters of the middle and south forks of the Yuba River, Meadow Lake was dammed by the South Yuba Canal Company in 1858 in order to divert water for their foothill mining operations. In 1860, Henry H. Hartley, an Englishman suffering from tuberculosis, built a small cabin near the lake and settled in . For three years, Hartley lived the life of a hermit. He survived the harsh winters by trapping and skiing over the deep snow on "Norwegian snow-skates," precursor to the modern ski. For Hartley, the rigors of mountain life improved his health.

In June, 1863, he discovered some reddish, gold-bearing rock a half-mile southeast of the lake. Two other miners, John Simons and Henry Feutel, soon joined Hartley as partners. When the three men located two promising, fifteen foot wide ledges of decomposed gold-bearing ore, they quietly formed the Excelsior Mining Company. It took another year for the word to leak of the gold strike at Meadow Lake, but in the spring of 1865, hundreds of unemployed hard-rock miners, entrepreneurs, and businessmen on the financially depressed

Comstock rushed to the remote lake. By June at least three thousand people had abandoned Virginia City for the "excitement" at Meadow Lake. Hartley, Feutel, and Simons were overwhelmed by the sheer number of people crowding their Excelsior claim. Within a few weeks, twelve hundred new mining sites had been legally recorded and scores of paper claims littered the rocky slopes.

In the spring of 1866, four thousand more people joined the Meadow Lake gold rush. Residents spoke of civic improvements and sites were selected for a new church and school. Hartley's Excelsior Company was breaking ground for a new twelve-stamp mill. Land parcels that had sold for $25 the year before were now selling like hotcakes for $1,500 to $2,000 each, payable in gold coin. By the end of the 1866 summer mining season, there were six hundred new buildings at Meadow Lake, including a church meeting house and sturdy brick bank. There were three large hotels packed with customers day and night. Ninety saloons slaked the thirst of the hard-working miners. Painted courtesans lounged in the saloons, drinking whiskey and smoking cigars. A small double-decked steamer cruised the shallow waters of Meadow Lake. On Saturday nights, the miners boarded the steamer for excursions to the upper end of the lake where four hurdy-gurdy houses sheltered prostitutes.

In the following summer of 1867, there were eight large mills with a total of seventy-two ore-crushing stamps in operation. Despite all the mining activity there was precious little money being made. The ore around Meadow Lake generated assays of $50 to $100 per ton, but there was a problem with the milling process that had everyone stumped. The obdurate ore refused to yield to the common reduction processes known at the time. It seemed that a strange mixture of arsenic, antimony, lead and other metals rendered their usual methods of amalgamation by mercury useless. Countless tests and many attempts at every known European milling method could not free the gold and silver from the matrix. In frustration, some of the baffled miners even tried a process that some charlatan dreamed up; it too failed. One old miner commented cautiously, "There is gold in there, plenty of it; only it is not gold as gold."

Although the Meadow Lake population soared again in the summer of 1867, much of the excitement for a big strike had withered away. The metallurgical conundrum sounded the death knell of the remote mining camp. Within just a few weeks, the disillusioned began a massive exodus back to Washoe or California. One articulate observer wrote, "One by one, all the miserable riffraff, the indolent, worthless, and profligate adventurers, who have no capital, no industry, no brains, and who expect to make their living by fleecing honest men; all the gamblers and the harlots; the old prospectors, weather-beaten and grizzled; the young greenhorns, without the means to procure a meal of victuals; all the lily-livered counter-jumpers; all the thieves, pickpockets, and roughs, were gone." The "honest miners" followed the social parasites. They shouldered their picks and shovels, many of them muttering bitter words about "Hartley's Folly." In short, Meadow Lake was abandoned except for a few hard-headed and desperate men who clung to the last straw of hope. Eventually, the only person to remain was Henry Hartley, the eccentric and adventurous Englishman who had first settled there. Over the next twenty years, Hartley, the last true believer, bought up and consolidated all the Meadow Lake claims into his own single holding.

Occasionally during the summer, a prospector or two might give Meadow Lake a quick look-over, but only Hartley stayed through the deep winter snows. A curious resident of

Grass Valley skied up to the ghostly mining camp in the winter of 1872-73. On twelve-foot-long skis he glided through its empty streets, level with the second story windows. The silence was eerie. He skied past the vacant office of the *Meadow Lake Morning Sun* newspaper, once a busy daily. Peering through the upper floor windows of one fancy hotel, he could see tidy rooms furnished with chairs, washstands, mirrors and beds with clean linen, still waiting for guests that would never arrive.

In September 1873, a transient lit a fire in the Excelsior Hotel, which spread through the dilapidated ghost town. The flames swept through Meadow Lake's wooden shacks, sparing only a few. Hartley, however, continued to stay at the abandoned camp, living in the last remaining house, surrounded by fancy furnishings that he had salvaged before the fire. Hartley's dream of riches finally came true in November 1891, when a syndicate of French investors offered him big money for the mining claims. But fate intervened and Hartley died unexpectedly while preparing for his journey to Europe. Henry Hartley, was buried on a wooded hill west of the lake, "the last man in an ephemeral city he helped create."

Shortly after the 1892 death of Henry Hartley, his estranged wife Alice showed up to claim her husband's estate. Henry had held legal title to the failed Meadow Lake gold mines for nearly thirty years in hope that he would strike it rich one day. Ironically, he died shortly after the consortium of European investors agreed in principle to pay him handsomely for his mining rights. Alice had been in Italy studying art and music when she heard of her husband's death. Anticipating a large cash inheritance from the Meadow Lake claims, she returned as quickly as possible and rented several rooms at Grass Valley's finest hotel. Unfortunately, the worthless mining stocks and

$1,500 left by her impoverished husband barely covered her debts.

Henry Hartley was fifty-three-years-old when he met Alice back in May 1886. The hermit was buying supplies at Cisco, California, on the Central Pacific's main track west of Donner Summit. Alice was a lovely young women, nearly half his age. But she had a secret past; her infant baby from an unknown relationship had just died that spring. If Henry knew, he didn't care. It was lonely at Meadow Lake. They both hailed from England and separately had traveled to the Sierra mountains to recover from chronic respiratory conditions. Hartley, whose first wife had died in 1882, impressed Alice as a wealthy mining magnate and the couple married in Sierraville a year later. Their relationship was short-lived, however. After only a few weeks at Hartley's remote mining camp at Meadow Lake, his socially-inclined wife fled to Grass Valley. When Hartley arrived to fetch her home a loud argument erupted and the newlyweds split up. Hartley returned to Meadow Lake and Alice moved to Virginia City.

She later sailed for Europe where she enjoyed the life of an artist. It wasn't until Henry's death in 1892, that Alice returned to the United States. After settling her affairs at Meadow Lake, Alice moved to Reno in September 1893. Nevada's desert climate improved her asthma condition and it was relatively close to her mining claim at Meadow Lake. Alice still hoped to profit from the mines, she just couldn't live there. Mrs. Hartley rented an apartment-studio on the third floor of the imposing Bank of Nevada where she offered art lessons and classes to the public. Supporting herself by selling some of the Meadow Lake claims, she joined Reno's social elite and applied for the position of art teacher in the Reno schools. The Honorable Murray D. Foley was president of the Bank of Nevada and a Nevada state senator. The handsome senator and the recently-widowed Alice were introduced by a mutual friend during a railroad excursion to Boca, California. Thirty-year-old Alice was described as "...prepossessing in appearance, always dressed neatly and in good taste, is well-educated, a good conversationalist and bright and vivacious." Foley was smitten.

In December someone showed Sen. Foley some promising samples of ore gold taken from Alice's moribund mines at Meadow Lake and offered to act as a broker in order to sell the claims. Sen. Foley began calling on Alice to discuss a possible transaction of the claim. Late in the evening, on January 13, 1894, Foley arrived unannounced at Alice's apartment. According to Alice, Foley asked her to join him for a late supper—which she refused. Alice charged that the senator secretly drugged her brandy. When she regained her senses, Foley was beside her in bed. After the assault, Lady Alice refused any further meetings with Mr. Foley and had the locks on her studio doors changed. Despite her precautions, on the evening of February 26, she returned home to find the obsessed politician hiding in her apartment. Once more he forced her to submit to his will. Alice bought a gun the next day and threatened to shoot the senator if he attacked her again. Foley must have believed her because from then on he avoided her.

Shortly after the second assault, Alice took several of her paintings to San Francisco, where they received favorable critical review. In late March, Alice realized that she was pregnant. When she confronted Senator Foley in his office, he insisted on an abortion. Foley forced her to visit a San Francisco abortionist, but the physician advised against the procedure for health reasons. Alice decided that she wanted to keep the child. In May she retained Reno attorney, E. R. Dodge, whose office was just below her studio in the Bank of Nevada building. She had Dodge write up a legal document acknowl-

edging Foley's paternity and establishing financial responsibility for her and the child. Unaware that she was consulting with a lawyer located in his own building, Senator Foley feigned cooperation and agreed to draft a letter of financial support and place it on the record in Salt Lake City where Alice intended to relocate. The couple did not meet again until July 26 when she called Senator Foley to her apartment to tell him she was leaving Reno for Salt Lake City. Foley, married with children, admitted that no legal papers had been filed and that she and the child were on their own.

A heated argument ensued at which point Alice told Foley that she had consulted with the attorney Dodge. Foley, described as "about six feet in height, broad shouldered, deep chested, and of herculean build" went berserk. He jumped up and struck her in the shoulder threatening "...if you make trouble for me I will buy some men with a few twenty dollar gold pieces to testify to anything." He then grabbed a heavy chair and swung it at her. Alice quickly seized her Colt revolver and shot two .38 caliber bullets into Senator Foley. He dropped the chair and gasped, "that settles it, it has gone through me." He stumbled down the steps, mortally wounded. On the floor below, he barged into the office of Dr. P. T. Phillips where he collapsed on the examination couch. Foley gasped, "Doctor, I am shot and a dead man." Another physician joined Dr. Phillips but there was nothing they could do. Murray Foley was unconscious in ten minutes and dead in thirty. His faithful wife reached his side just as he died. While the doctors did their best to save the senator's life, Alice Hartley slipped past and quickly entered her attorney's office. Still gripping the pistol, Alice told Dodge, "I have killed Senator Foley, or at least I shot him and hope he is dead."

An impressive funeral was held in Reno on July 29, 1894. The parade to Mountain View Cemetery was led by the town band, Reno Guard and many Nevada dignitaries. At the gravesite, a bugler played Taps and the militia fired a twenty-one gun salute. Eulogies by Foley's wife and political cronies described the murdered senator as "an enterprising citizen...large-hearted and generous." Murray D. Foley was practically regarded as a saint. In 1891, historian Hubert H. Bancroft wrote, "Mr. Foley ...has the most profound regard for the wholesome moral teachings of the Christian doctrine, and to the needy or unfortunate is ever ready to extend a helping hand." Only after the ceremonies did the truth about Senator Foley's ugly character reveal itself. Nevada newspapers later acknowledged Foley's womanizing. Described as "a professional libertine," editors wondered publicly how the senator had avoided vengeful husbands or fathers, since Foley often boasted of his amorous affairs to barroom buddies. In fact, his friends had always expected him to die that way.

Sen. Foley's wife confirmed the charges by refusing to hang black crepe on the family home and she quickly left for San Francisco with her husband's $250,000 estate. The murder trial lasted several days and was front page news. The prosecution portrayed pregnant Alice as a "dangerous and intriguing woman" with a history of easy virtue. Defense attorney Dodge used Alice as his only witness and made a strong case for self-defense. Alice offered one day of testimony and endured two days of intense cross-examination by District Attorney Benjamin F. Curler. The all-male jury found Alice Hartley guilty of second-degree murder, but strongly recommended mercy. Despite the jury's desire for leniency, the judge sentenced her to eleven years in the Nevada State Prison. Crushed by the verdict, Alice told the jury, "Gentlemen, I thank you; I had hoped that you would exonerate me."

Two months later, on November 15, Alice gave birth to a son, Vernon Harrison Hartley. Legal maneuvers and appeals delayed her sentencing until January 12, 1895, when the court decreed that the defendant serve all eleven years. Attorney Dodge appealed to a higher court. On May 22, the Nevada Supreme Court sustained the lower court's conviction. Two weeks later, Alice and her baby were taken to the State Prison at Carson City, where they were lodged near the guard's quarters outside the prison walls. But the citizens of Nevada did not want a nursing mother and infant in their State Prison. Finally, after numerous petitions to the Board of Pardons, she was freed after serving eighteen months of her sentence. Released on January 12, 1897, Mrs. Hartley returned to Reno and filed a law suit in the District Court for her son's share of the Foley estate. Tragically, the boy died of scarlet fever just seven weeks later.

Broken-hearted, Alice Hartley moved to San Francisco where she suffered a nervous breakdown. Believing that God had told her to repent, she sometimes interrupted Sunday services by seizing the pulpit to shock the congregation with grim details of Foley's killing. In January 1899, the *San Francisco Chronicle* reported that Mrs. Alice Hartley had married William S. Bonnifield, a twice-divorced lawyer from Winnemucca. William was the nephew of Supreme Court Judge Bonnifield, a member of the Board of Pardons that had released Alice from prison two years before. The marriage lasted less than two weeks, however, and Bonnifield returned to Winnemucca alone. Nothing seemed to work for Alice.

With nothing but the remaining Meadow Lake mining stocks to support her, Alice turned to crime. In 1907, she was caught stealing jewels in San Francisco. To evade prosecution she fled over Donner Pass and continued east to Denver where she fell ill and died on New Year's Day, 1908. Through little fault of her own, Alice Hartley is remembered as the only person to kill a sitting Nevada state senator. Alice may have pulled the trigger, but she wasn't alone in the general desire to rid society of Murray D. Foley. Among the many petitions Nevadans submitted to the Board of Pardons in their effort to free Alice, was a list signed by more than sixty prominent citizens. Instead of imprisonment, they demanded the State give her a gold medal for the deed.

CHAPTER FIVE SELECTED SOURCES

John M. Townley, *Tough Little Town on the Truckee (1868 – 1900),* Great Basin Studies Center, Reno, Nevada, 1983.

W. B. Lardner & M. J. Brock, *History of Placer and Nevada Counties, California,* Historic Record Company, Los Angeles, CA, 1924.

Hubert Howe Bancroft, *History of Nevada, Colorado, and Wyoming,* San Francisco History Company, San Francisco, CA, 1890.

Clarence M. Wooster, *Meadow Lake City and Winter at Cisco in the Sixties,* California Historical Society Quarterly, Volume XVIII, San Francisco, CA, 1939.

Anne M. Butler, *Gendered Justice in the American West; Women Prisoners in Men's Penitentiaries,* University of Illinois Press, Chicago, IL 1997.

Stephen Powers, *A City of a Day,* Overland Monthly Magazine, July – December, 1874.

William Banks Berry, *The Lost Sierra; Gold, Ghosts & Skis,* Western SkiSport Museum, Soda Springs, California, 1991.

The Journals of Alfred Doten (1849 – 1903), Edited by Walter Van Tilburg Clark, Volume Three, University of Nevada Press, Reno, Nevada, 1973.

Hubert Howe Bancroft, *Chronicle of the Builders, San Francisco, Volume VII,* The History Company, San Francisco, CA, 1891.

Phillip I. Earl, *The Hartley-Foley Murder Case,* Nevada Historical Society's "This Was Nevada" series, published in *Reno Gazette-Journal,* April 1, 1990.

Meadow Lake Morning Sun, June 6, 1866.

Sacramento Union, March 30, April 20, May 11, 1866; March 29, 1867; December 23, 1868, September 22, 1883; November 4, 1891.

Nevada State Journal, July & September, 1894.

Reno Evening Gazette, July & September, 1894.

Reese River Reveille, November 24, 1883; April 15, 1887; January 10, 1894.

Carson City Daily Appeal, July & September, 1894 & January 2, 1908.

San Francisco Chronicle, July 27 & July 28, 1894.

Meadow Lake Mill and Mining Co., (1865 – 1866), Archive Manuscript, California State Library, Boxes 854 – 855.

Julia Bulette: Queen of D Street

THE DAY SHE DIED, the hard-rock miners of Virginia City cried a river of tears. The vicious strangling of thirty-five-year-old Julia Bulette on January 20, 1867, stunned residents on the Comstock. Julia may have been a prostitute, but that didn't stop the citizenry from organizing an impressive funeral for their favorite "fair but frail" lady of the evening.

Julia Bulette was born in London in 1832. As a young girl she emigrated to New Orleans where she later married a man named Smith. When their relationship soured, Julia joined the California Gold Rush in 1852; but she had no intentions of panning for gold in California. Miss Bulette earned a living as a prostitute in numerous mining camps for nearly a decade before the silver excitement in the Nevada mines drew her to Virginia City in April 1863. The Comstock boom was barely four years old in 1863, but there were already thousands of young, single miners there, most of them about twenty years old. The Virginia City census of 1860 reported a population of 2,390, of whom only 118 were women. The Comstock had the busiest saloons in the West. Liquor flowed freely and the miners' boisterous behavior was legend. Virginia City is built on the side of a mountain, centered around C Street as Commercial Row. On the streets above, new millionaires built mansions. Prostitutes, working men, and unmarried miners lived below on D Street. Prostitution was the single largest occupation for women on the Comstock. At a time when laundry or domestic pay was less than $25 per month, many women turned to prostitution in a desperate attempt to pay their bills. Although some members in the community looked down on prostitution, the mere presence of women had a soothing effect upon the predominantly male society. On miner claimed, "Many's the miner who'd never wash his face or comb his hair, if he wasn't thinkin' of the sportin' girls he might meet in the saloons." Julia Bulette moved into a small frame house at No. 4 D Street, in Virginia City's red-light district. In 1861, Nevada Territory had adopted the English Common law that deemed brothels public nuisances but not illegal. Although her cottage was small, Julia decorated it tastefully with comfortable mahogany furniture, imported carpets, and lace curtains. For her customer's enjoyment, Julia stocked a small bar with whiskey, port, claret, and rum. In her bedroom she had a wash-basin and spittoon, as well as a steamer trunk for her fancy dresses. Her large bed was shielded by heavy curtains. It was a state of luxury that none of the other women on the "row" enjoyed.

Julia's reputation as an attractive, kind-hearted and generous woman grew rapidly. So many men desired her attention that the "Queen of D Street" could pick and choose her clients at will. Independent, middle class prostitutes like Julia Bulette usually entertained only one man a night. Many of her customers were wealthy gentlemen who gave her expensive gifts of jewelry and furs. Although venereal disease was common among prostitutes, Julie Bulette kept her health by visiting the doctor almost everyday. Testament to her acceptance by the respectable community was her successful election as an honorary member of the Virginia Engine Company No. 1, the city's elite firefighters. The department consisted of the energetic men in town who thrilled to the excitement and exertion inherent in fighting dangerous fires. The cream of the community, these men were leading stockbrokers, merchants and speculators. Julia's generous financial gifts to

the fire department helped them purchase the most modern equipment.

Virginia City is built of wood and perched on a wind-swept mountainside. Sparks from wood burning stoves frequently set the city on fire. To protect the town, Company No. 1 was equipped with one of the most powerful engines on the Pacific Coast. It was armed with six hundred feet of hose and manned by sixty-five men. When the brave men of Company No. 1 raced to a fire, it was usually Julia Bulette working the brakes as they rounded a corner or pulled to an abrupt stop. In late 1866, Julia fell ill and was confined to her bed for several months. She moved to Carson City in order to rest until she felt better. She returned to her cottage on D Street in January 1867.

On Saturday night, January 19, Julia dressed and went to see a performance at the Opera House. Prostitutes were required to sit in a special viewing box with the curtains tightly closed, so the "proper ladies" in town did not have to see the "working girls." When proud Julia refused to sit in the section reserved for women from the red light district, she was denied admission to the theater. Miss Bulette returned to D Street to eat dinner and visit with her next-door neighbor and friend, Gertrude Holmes. At 11:30 p.m., Julia said good-night to Gertrude and returned to her own home. Julia must have been exhausted because her clothes were later found in a pile by the bed, as if she had just dropped them there and crawled under the covers. When Gertrude delivered Sunday breakfast the following morning, she found Julia Bulette brutally murdered. She had been struck with the hammer of a pistol, bludgeoned with a thick piece of firewood, and then strangled. Imprints from the assailant's fingers and thumbs were still visible on her throat. Most of her finer jewelry, furs and clothing were missing. The town was shocked into sobriety by the violent act, and the citizenry demanded a prompt search for the killer or killers. The *Gold Hill Evening News* insisted on an immediate hanging as soon as the culprit was caught.

On Monday, January 21, Julia Bulette's funeral was held at Engine House No. 1 on B Street. It was a bitterly cold day, with gusty winds and blinding snow. Despite the adverse weather, many turned out to hear the Reverend William Martin's eulogy. Extolling the virtues of a known prostitute is not easy for a man of the cloth, but Rev. Martin's sermon was well-received and considered to be "most appropriate to the occasion." The Virginia City *Territorial Enterprise* described her as "being of a very kind-hearted, liberal, benevolent and charitable disposition — few of her class had more true friends."

Her fellow firefighters in Engine Company No. 1, took up a collection and purchased a handsome silver-handled casket. After the sermon, the Metropolitan Brass Band led about sixty members of the fire department on foot as well as sixteen carriages of mourners to the Flowery Hill Cemetery. Attendance would have been greater but the vicious winter storm and muddy roads kept many at home. Although Julia was given a Catholic funeral, the populace could not let a woman of easy virtue be buried in consecrated ground. She was entombed in a lonely grave half a mile east of town. A simple wooden plank with the name "Julia" painted on it was all that marked her final resting place. As the mourners slowly filed back into town, the men of Engine Co. No.1 sang "The Girl I Left Behind." Virginia City was draped in black, and for the first time since Lincoln's assassination, all the saloons were closed in respect for the somber mood. Although Julia's few remaining belongings had little value, her creditors offered a $200 reward for the killer's capture. A few months later, prostitute Martha Camp was awakened by someone approaching her with a weapon. Her screams sent the man fleeing in panic, but she later recognized him on the street. He was identified as Jean Marie A. Villain, commonly known as John Millian, a French baker and drifter. Millian was quickly arrested and thrown in jail. On May 24, four months after the crime, Mrs. Cazentre of Gold Hill reported that she had purchased a $40 dress from Millian. Sam Rosener, a dry goods merchant in Virginia City, recognized it as one he had ordered and sold to Julia Bulette. The next day, a thorough search of Millian's house and storage trunk at the bakery revealed many of Julia Bulette's possessions.

Alf Doten, editor of the *Gold Hill Evening News,* wrote in his diary; "The murderer of Julia Bulette is now in the county jail. This evening the chief visited him in his cell and showed him the evidences of his guilt. The fellow wilted and finally confessed – said two other men helped him murder her. This creates great excitement in this city. Murder will out." Millian's trial began on July 2, 1867. Among the witnesses for the prosecution were Mrs. Cazentre and Sam Rosener who identified Julia Bulette's dress. Other witnesses included the famous stagecoach driver, Hank Monk, who identified the rings, watches and other items found in Millian's possession. At the trial Millian retracted his confession and his defense attorney, Charles De Long, argued that the entire case was based on circumstantial evidence. But given all the evidence against him, the jury quickly convicted Millian of murder in the first degree. Three days later Millian was sentenced to be hanged. Despite the conviction, De Long wasn't ready to give up on his client. He appealed the case to the State Supreme Court, but the justices upheld the lower court's decision. De Long, who had fought hard for his client, later said, "No skill or eloquence could successfully battle against the terrible evidences of guilt that surrounded the doomed man." Some nine months after the trial, John Millian was escorted from the

Storey County Jail to the gallows located about a mile north of Virginia City.

In the moments before the noose was placed around his neck, John Millian gave his final statement. In broken English the condemned man spoke: "Mr. Hall and family, I am very much obliged to you for your services and also to the kind ladies that visited me in my cell." A few women in town believed that the removal of prostitute Julia Bulette was good for the city. They had brought food to the prisoner while he was in custody and had circulated a petition requesting that his sentence be commuted to life imprisonment. Their efforts to save Millian's life failed, however, and just before one o'clock in the afternoon on April 24, 1868, nearly three thousand onlookers watched Millian drop to his death. The brutal murder of Julia Bulette had finally been avenged.

CHAPTER SEVEN SELECTED SOURCES

Cathy Luchetti & Carol Olwell, *Women of the West,* The Library of the American West, Orion Books, New York, NY, 1982.

Paula Mitchell Marks, *Precious Dust: The True Saga of the Western Gold Rushes,* HarperCollins *West,* New York NY, 1994.

Elizabeth Margo, *Women of the Gold Rush,* Indian Head Books, New York, NY, 1955.

Douglas McDonald, *The Legend of Julia Bulette and the Red Light Ladies of Nevada,* Nevada Publications, Las Vegas, Nevada, 1983.

Anne Seagraves, *Soiled Doves: Prostitution in the Early West,* WESANNE PUBLICATIONS, Hayden, Idaho, 1994.

Anne Seagraves, *Women of the Sierra,* WESANNE Enterprises, Lakeport, California, 1990.

Guy Louis Rocha, *Nevada's Most Peculiar Industry: Brothel Prostitution, Its Land Use Implications and its Relationship to the Community,* State Archivist, Nevada State Library & Archives. Presentation to Nevada State Planning Conference, Carson Valley Inn, Minden, Nevada on November 9, 1993.

John M. Townley, *Little Town on the Truckee: Reno 1868 – 1900,* Great Basin Studies Center, Reno, Nevada, 1983.

Journals of Alfred Doten 1849 – 1903, edited by Walter Van Tilburg Clark, University of Nevada Press, Reno, Nevada, 1973.

Charles De Long, *Life and Confession of John Millian: Murderer of Julia Bulette,* Lammon, Gregory & Palmer, Virginia City, Nevada, 1868.

Mrs. Hugh Brown, *Lady in Boomtown: Miners and Manners on the Nevada Frontier,* University of Nevada Press, Reno, Nevada, 1968.

William R. Gillis, *Gold Rush Days with Mark Twain,* Albert & Charles Boni Publishing, New York, NY, 1930.

Virginia City *Territorial Enterprise,* January 22, 1867

Gold Hill Evening News, January 21, 1867.

Sacramento Bee, January 10, 1868.

PHOTO CREDITS

Page 79   Julia Bulette, *Courtesy Nevada Historical Society.*

Captain Barter: Hermit of Emerald Bay

8

WEST OF SOUTH LAKE TAHOE is a spectacular, glacially-scoured basin known as the Desolation Wilderness. Scalloped in eons past by flowing ice, the polished granite now cradles countless alpine lakes. For the hardy hiker, Desolation is a region of sublime beauty. Towering above the shattered cliffs and glacial debris looms Dick's Peak, elevation 9,974 feet, standing stoic and solitary in this region of rugged extremes. The obdurate mountain is a fitting monument to Captain Richard Barter, a man whose remarkable feats of survival have withstood the test of time.

A retired British sea captain, Dick Barter shipped into Tahoe when he was hired by the son of famous stager, Ben Holladay. Holladay, known as the Stagecoach King, was one of the wealthiest men in the West. His stage line ran two thousand miles, from the Mississippi River all the way to Placerville, California. The most direct overland route to the California gold fields passed through South Lake Tahoe.

Tahoe was originally named by the indigenous Washoe natives. In 1880, Dr. Henry De Groot visited the lake with a Washoe tribal leader. He told Dr. De Groot that the Indians call this water "*Tah-hoe-ee*," meaning big lake or water. "*Ta*" is the Washoe root for "water" and "*tah-oo* or *ta-au* means "lake water" or "sheet of water." Tahoe has also been known by other names. When John Fremont first sighted this beautiful body of water in 1844, he christened it Lake Bonpland, after Aimé Jacques Alexandre Bonpland, a French naturalist. In 1851 the lake was changed to Bigler, in honor of California governor, John Bigler. The original Tahoe name is now official and permanent, but Ben Holladay was not concerned with the lake's changing nomenclature. He was stunned by its beauty. In 1862, Holladay spent a few days exploring the lake. His favorite spot was a magical little inlet called Eagle Bay, re-named Emerald Bay in 1874, famed for the American eagles nesting there. Never one to hesitate, the "Napoleon of the Plains" pre-empted the unoccupied land surrounding the pic-turesque bay. On a small plateau at the foot of Bald Eagle Mountain, Holladay built a two-story, five-room villa. Pri-marily a summer residence, he called it "The Cottage." Rock-bordered paths led to nearby Eagle Falls, and a "Willow Walk" led to a large boathouse and wharf where several small skiffs were moored. It was the first private estate constructed on Lake Tahoe.

In 1863 the Stagecoach King turned the property over to his son, Ben Holladay, Jr., who hired Captain Richard Barter to take care of the estate during the harsh winter months. The decision to employ an old sea captain to keep a remote moun-tain mansion ship-shape was pure logic. When deep snow blanketed the Sierra, the only way in or out of the bay was by boat. To manage an estate at storm-swept Emerald Bay, the caretaker had to be seaworthy. Captain Barter was the right man for the job.

Sometimes pioneers who visited snowbound Lake Tahoe during the winter could not resist sporting a joke on their fellow flatlanders. In the 1870s, the Carson City *Appeal* pub-lished a fish story that reeks of 19th century mining humor. In an article titled, "Trout Mining at Lake Bigler," the editor wrote, "In the general freeze which has converted the lake into a sea of ice, Emerald Bay has been frozen solid. It is one vast ledge of ice from the surface of its transparent waters to the bottom. From some cause best known to themselves, the fish, especially the trout, have fairly swarmed here. When the great and sudden freezing came it imprisoned them by hundreds of tons all over the bay. There they are fixed like a bee in a drop of amber."

Hank Monk, a popular, yarn-spinning stagecoach driver, took the story one step further. Monk stated that several men were chopping tunnels through the thick ice in Emerald Bay between the boat landing and Cap'n Dick's Island, and actually mining the imprisoned trout by the cartload. Hank swore that he had an interest in one of the "mining claims" and he expected prompt and numerous dividends. Folklore permeates Tahoe history, but the story of Captain Dick is no tall tale. For twelve years, this British salt lived the life of a recluse at Ben Holladay's isolated cottage. Holladay accumulated his vast fortune by running his stage company with a tight fiscal fist, and the Stagecoach King's financial success merited little respect from the general populace.

Locally, Captain Dick's employment with the Holladay empire earned him the sobriquet "Hero of Robber's Roost." Life at Emerald Bay was full of hardship and danger. When asked about the depth of snow there during the winter of 1869-70, Captain Barter said, "Along towards spring it stood about thirteen feet on a level. But then, you know," he added apologetically, "that was an uncommonly mild winter." After each winter storm, massive avalanches thundered down the steep mountainsides. Captain Dick once described his harsh living conditions to a visiting San Francisco reporter: "The winter before last I was on top of my kitchen throwin' snow from the roof four feet to the level above my head. Suddenly I heard something a-crackling away up there..." and Barter pointed toward the summit of Granite Mountain that rose 3,000 feet above his little shack near the cottage. The old sailor continued his story, "Looking up, I saw everything a-breaking loose from their fastenings and coming down the mountain hoppity-jump. Yes sir, everything, pine trees, big boulders, snow and all a-coming down together. They was making right for me and I thought Old Gabriel called me sure enough so I just dropped my shovel and waited. But sir, my time hadn't come yet for up yonder it struck a granite ridge and slewed off, clearing me by about ten feet, and plunged right into the bay, sending the water up hundreds of feet."

Captain Dick was a real-life Robinson Crusoe. In order to retain his sanity, the old shellback related personally to the wilderness that surrounded him. He told his rare summer visitors that when his solitary existence began to wear him down, he would walk over to the Eagle Falls cascade and sit beside the rushing waterfall. He said, "Whenever I am down-hearted, I come out here and talk to it. It's Old Gabriel's voice to me, and tells me all I want to know." When asked whether he ever had any problems with grizzly bears, he responded, "Yes, I hears 'em around my house every once in a while, but as I ain't lost no grizzly, I don't never go out to find none! This 'ere place is big enough for both of us to live in without bothering each other."

The old captain possessed a fatalistic spirituality. He believed that "Old Gabriel" was close to calling him home to heaven. When he was asked about growing old alone at Emerald Bay, the hermit said, "Somehow or other, I feel that my time to die is drawing near—so I am going to make a coffin, hang the lid on hinges, and put it in position in the cave, so that when I feel that I am called, I'll just come out here, get in this coffin, shut down the lid, and then, goodbye Old Dick. All they have to do when they come is just pile up the stones at the mouth of the cave. You see, the first one that might come by could be young Ben, my master, and you know it wouldn't be nice for him to find me dead in my 'ouse and

smelling bad!" But it would take more than destructive avalanches, roaming grizzly bears and fierce winters storms before the old captain answered Gabriel's trumpet call.

Captain Barter lived a life of isolation and visitors to Emerald Bay were rare. Despite his eccentric lifestyle, the venerable sailor gained a reputation as an easygoing old salt who enjoyed the taste of bourbon whiskey. When "Uncle Dick" was drinking at the bar, customers were treated to ribald tales from his seafaring days. If Barter craved a drink during the snowbound winter, he sailed for it. It was sixteen miles from Emerald Bay to William Pomin's Tahoe House Saloon in Tahoe City, and a risky voyage in a small boat. But neither distance nor danger deterred Barter's efforts to reach his favorite watering hole. One cold January night Barter nearly met "Old Gabriel." Captain Dick told the story eight months later when a reporter from the San Francisco *Daily Alta Californian* visited him at his cottage. The hermit greeted the journalist and his boatman with a loaded derringer in each hand, but when Barter saw the bottle of whisky that his visitors had thoughtfully brought, he welcomed them with open arms.

After a few drinks, the captain regaled the newspaperman with stories about his life at Emerald Bay: "On the 26th day of January 1870, I was at Tahoe City, and had imbibed so freely that I thought I had better leave there, so about eight o'clock at night I got into my little boat and started for home. I had got no more than five or six miles, when in a sudden gust, my boat upset, precipitating me into the water. After struggling for some time, I succeeded in gaining a hold upon my boat, which after much exertion, I righted. The night was of inky blackness, and the weather intensely cold, the mercury being many degrees below zero." (January 1870 was dryer than normal, but also unusually cold.) The old skipper continued, "I knew it was useless to call for help, for on that wide expanse of water, there was not a human being within reach of my voice. I also knew that if I got into my boat and attempted to reach shore, I should certainly freeze to death." Captain Barter had capsized two miles off Sugar Pine Point. He realized that his only chance of survival was to remain in the water. He tied the boat's bowline around his chest and began swimming south towards Emerald Bay, ten miles away. Fortunately for the struggling sailor, his bottle of whisky floated within reach. The slugs of alcohol numbed the pain of the chilling water. He was sixty-three years old but unwilling to answer the angel Gabriel's call just yet. After two hours in the frigid water fighting the waves, he climbed back into the little dinghy and wrapped himself in some wet blankets. All night he sculled against the biting wind and freezing spray, shouting, "Richard Barter never surrenders! Richard Barter never surrenders!" Barter's grim determination saved his life.

The half-frozen sailor rowed into Emerald Bay at daybreak. But his ordeal was far from over: "And so, after many hours' labor, I reached my landing, crawled into this house, and for eleven weeks I never left; 'cause you see, my feet and one hand was froze and I couldn't get out." Though seriously hurt, the old captain wasn't idle. During his three month confinement, Barter meticulously crafted a seven-foot miniature model of a man-o'-war steam frigate. It was a marvel of workmanship. Every rope, block, and sail was in its proper place; the running gear and propeller were driven by a wind-up clock hidden in the hold. On the deck of the wooden vessel stood 225 crew members, officers, marines, boatswains, and sailors, all hand-carved from small pieces of wood. The figures were painted to represent various styles of dress; indeed, no two of them had the same facial countenance. When Captain Barter pushed back the doors to the miniature galley, two Lilliputian cooks were standing in front of a cooking range topped with kitchen utensils made of perfectly shaped burnished copper.

It was an amazing feat, but not the only project that the self-reliant recluse completed that winter. Captain Dick couldn't walk on his injured feet, so he tied a small cushion to each knee in order to get around. While in this awkward condition, he gathered the lumber for, built, and then rigged a full-sized boat. No small-scale replica, this ship weighed four tons. He christened it *Nancy* and launched it by himself. Not a single person had visited throughout the whole winter.

At this point in the story, Captain Barter could see that the journalist was a bit skeptical about his survival story. The miniature model and four-ton ship were ample physical evidence of the captain's industry, but had he really experienced that near-fatal ordeal last winter? Barter limped over to a dressing table in Holladay's cottage and removed a small jewelry box. He lifted the lid and handed it to the newspaperman. "Them's my toes!" Captain Dick exclaimed proudly. Inside the little box were the captain's frostbitten toes that he had amputated and then salted to preserve as a memento of his fearful night on Lake Tahoe. The bemused reporter was convinced. When the bottle of whiskey was empty, it was time to go. The journalist later wrote, "When we left, the old man hated to see us go as he didn't know when he would see anybody again and his last words to us were that he would probably answer Gabriel's call … shortly."

Captain Barter knew that his luck on Tahoe wouldn't last forever. The old sailor chose the little island in the middle of Emerald Bay for his burial and final resting place. Capt. Barter first built a small "Island Cottage" on the edge of the granite isle, chiseled out a rocky tomb, and then erected a Gothic chapel over it. Gabriel finally came calling for Richard Barter

on October 18, 1873. The hermit had spent the evening drinking in Tom Rowland's Lake House Saloon at the south end of the lake. Ernest Pomin, one of five brothers from Alsace-Lorraine who were among the first to settle Tahoe City, was there at the saloon that night. He later wrote, "Captain Barter was sober for once when he made his final journey." But the old seaman was known for his capacity to drink bourbon and sobriety was a rare state for the good captain.

While Barter was sailing back to Emerald Bay in the *Nancy*, a sudden gale caught him by surprise. A gusty wind generated huge waves that broadsided the boat and drove it onto the rocks at Rubicon Point. Within minutes the small ship was smashed to pieces. Captain Barter escaped from the wreckage, but then drowned in 1,400 feet of water. Unfortunately, his earnest wish to be buried on his beloved island was thwarted since his body was never recovered from the deep water offshore. The hard drinking Englishman's love of whiskey had finally been his undoing. But in defense of the bottle, Captain Dick had once said, "Do you think, comrade, that a man can spend his life upon this pond (Tahoe), among these snow steeples, and not have a spree now and then? There's too much ice water in the Sierry's for a man to be a temperance chap. Who wants a dip across the lake in my *Nancy?* Trim a ship as ever rocked. Ho for Emerald Bay! Let's all drink...hurray!"

For years afterward, locals and tourists referred to the lovely little isle in Emerald Bay as Dead Man's Island. Today it is known as *Fannette Island*. *Fannette* is a corruption of *Coquette*, the moniker assigned by a group of young women and their male escorts who visited the island during the summer of 1866. The evidence of their visit was discovered in the 1880s, when a scribbled note inside an empty champagne bottle was found in a crevice on the island. To the prim Victorian ladies, the picturesque island of rock seemed like a coquettish flirt. On the note one had written, "The island appears to be in the center of a brilliant circle of admirers who, attracted by her beauty, still know she has a stony heart." The young men, who found the 150-foot-high granite island impossible to climb, agreed with the new name. One wrote, "the ways of this island, like those of an artful woman, are past finding out."

CHAPTER EIGHT SELECTED SOURCES

Edward B. Scott, *The Saga of Lake Tahoe,* Sierra-Tahoe Publishing Company, Crystal Bay, Lake Tahoe, Nevada, vol. I- 1957 & vol. II - 1973.

James V. Frederick, *Ben Holladay: The Stage Coach King,* The Arthur H. Clark Publishing Company, Glendale, California, 1940.

Carol Van Etten, *Tahoe City Yesterdays,* Sierra Maritime Publications, Lake Tahoe, 1987.

Helen S. Carlson, *Nevada Place Names: A Geographical Dictionary,* University of Nevada Press, Reno, Nevada, 1974.

Barbara Lekisch, *Tahoe Place Names,* Great West Books, Lafayette, CA, 1988.

San Francisco *Daily Alta Californian,* August 22, 1870 & January 10, 1878.

Truckee Republican, October 18, 1873.

Sacramento Union, May 29, 1875.

PHOTO CREDITS

Page 89   Captain Richard Barter's hand-carved ship, *Courtesy California State Library.*

Page 93   Captain Barter's Island Chapel in Emerald Bay, *Courtesy California State Library.*

The Vision of Crazy Sutro   9

THEY CALLED HIM CRAZY, but he contributed more to the success of the early West than all of his detractors combined. In San Francisco, the name Adolph Sutro stirs memories of the spectacular Sutro Heights and Cliff House, the cavernous Sutro Baths, or his election as a Populist mayor in 1894. But in the silver mining lore of Virginia City, Nevada, Sutro is associated with the Comstock Lode's famed Sutro Tunnel, a nineteenth century engineering marvel.

Adolph Heinrich Joseph Sutro, son of a wealthy clothing manufacturer, was born in Aachen, Germany, on April 29, 1830. As a boy, Adolph Sutro studied mechanics at a technical school in Prussia, and he held responsible positions in his family's textile mills while in his teens. The Sutro children enjoyed privileged lives in a twenty-room mansion until their father died following a tragic carriage accident. In 1850, Mrs. Sutro took all but one of her eleven children to America.

Young Adolph spent only one week in New York before gold fever struck and he booked passage on a California-bound steamer. Sutro shipped into San Francisco Bay on the steamer *California* on November 21, 1850. He had no money, but he planned to sell some fancy articles that he had purchased in Europe and brought along with him. The handsome twenty-year-old engineer was in for a major disappointment. Sutro's timing could not have been worse, for San Francisco was suffering from a serious fit of financial depression. The reckless miners had spent all their gold dust during the summer and were now holed up for the duration of the winter rains. They were more concerned with eating and drinking than buying fancy European soaps, perfumes and knick-knacks. Yet despite the lack of buyers, ships loaded with cargo continued to make port daily, and the warehouses bulged with unsold merchandise. The city's main economy had dried up for the season. Undaunted, Sutro displayed the persistent hustle that would become his trademark. Within two weeks, he had sold the merchandise and earned his profit. Twenty years later that same plucky perseverance would convince skeptical European investors to put up the necessary capital for the Sutro Tunnel. A friend said that in an argument Sutro "was as obstinate as two mules." Adolph Sutro didn't beat you, he wore you down.

Devastating urban firestorms destroyed San Francisco six times between 1849 and 1851. Once ignited, the searing flames would race like wildfire through the city's ramshackle wooden buildings. These raging infernos were started by a gang of arsonists known as the "Sydney Ducks," former prisoners from the penal colony in Sydney, Australia. This band of professional criminals methodically pillaged the shops and warehouses during the confusion caused by the firestorms they purposely started. Young Adolph soon found a position as a fire lookout. The owner of a glass and china boutique paid him to sleep on the floor of the shop at night and be on the alert for fire. If fire ever threatened the store, it was Sutro's job to battle the flames and discourage any potential looters. Fortunately, all was quiet under his watch, and Sutro was never called upon to display his fire- and hoodlum-fighting abilities.

Adolph Sutro's story of financial success and his historic legacy in the West began with a small-time tobacco store. Sutro worked hard and had a keen eye for business. By 1854, he owned three stores in San Francisco that specialized in the buying and selling of fine cigars. Sutro knew the market well and his sales among cigar-loving San Franciscans soared. In

the mid–1850s, Sutro obtained United States citizenship and married Leah Harris. Leah had no dreams of a life of grandeur, but her energetic husband did. In 1858, word of another gold strike in far-off British Columbia flashed across the Peninsula. His friends called him crazy, but the opportunistic Sutro saw the potential to make big money selling cigars and supplies to the miners up north. The main distribution point for the Fraser River gold district was the city of Victoria, B.C. Sutro bought a town lot there and opened his fourth tobacco and cigar store. The Fraser River gravel beds were loaded with "color," but there were more desperate prospectors than valuable nuggets. The strike was a bust.

The Fraser River fiasco forced Sutro's return to San Francisco, minus all the money he had invested in his latest pipe dream. In late 1859, the reckless excitement of another strike swept California. This time the new El Dorado was just over the Sierra Nevada in Utah Territory. Sutro, a self-made engineer, enjoyed the charm and excitement of San Francisco. But if he contented himself with his tobacco business there, he would never engineer anything more sophisticated than the business accounts at his stores. To raise money for his Nevada adventure, Sutro sold his stores, while Leah opened two lodging houses in downtown San Francisco. Restless as always, Sutro was on his way to the silver mines of Washoe country before the Sierra snowpack had melted. He tramped over snow-covered Carson Pass and stumbled down into the desert. From now on, the lure of the Comstock would never release Sutro's indomitable spirit, and despite his love for their six young children, Leah would forever be a Washoe Widow.

The ambitious tobacconist ersatz engineer arrived in Virginia City with every intention of carrying on his cigar business. One year later, so many miners had poured into the region that on March 2, 1861, Congress created Nevada Territory. As Sutro searched for a suitable storefront, he befriended a journeyman-reporter named Sam Clemens, who would succeed on his own as Mark Twain.

But it wasn't long before Sutro heard the siren call of his destiny. The frustrated engineer jumped into silver mining with both boots on. He entered the high stakes gamble by working with a German chemist to perfect the process of refining tailings — ore that had been through other mills and discarded as waste. The new system proved so successful that by 1863, Sutro was earning nearly $10,000 a month with the Nevada mill. Despite his breakthrough in ore processing, a greater challenge lay ahead for our cigar aficionado. Within the bowels of Virginia City's mountain of ore, the relentless digging had led to a stubborn stalemate. As the miners burrowed deeper into the earth, they inhaled filthy, foul-smelling air and breathing became nearly impossible. Candle wicks burned with a faint blue-green flame and at the deeper levels, the rocks heated to temperatures exceeding one hundred twenty degrees. Stripped to the waist, the exhausted miners were doused with cold water melted from Sierra snow, which was stocked in massive ice rooms. Each miner was allocated ninety-five pounds of ice per day. It barely kept them alive.

In order to vent the ever-deepening tunnels, huge canvas sails were rigged above the mines to harness the wind and funnel fresh air deep into the shafts. Later, giant pumps were designed, manufactured and then hauled over the Sierra from California by oxen-drawn wagon train. Ventilation wasn't the only problem. Working conditions had become deadly. Miners were now wielding their sharp picks in a danger zone. Thin seams of clay sealed off pockets of pressurized, super-heated water that ruptured with the slightest prick of the pick. Scalding-hot water would inundate the tunnel and trap the workmen. The most lucrative mines were soon flooded to many feet. Mining shares plummeted in value. Untold riches would go to the engineer who could solve the riddle of the Comstock. Adolph Sutro envisioned a horizontal tunnel bored into the base of Mount Davidson "which at once ensured drainage, ventilation, and facilitated the work." The tunnel would also be an escape route from fire or flood. Mine tailings and silver ore would be easily carted out on tracks through the tunnel instead of winching the ore up to the surface through vertical shafts and then hauling it by mule trains down steep roads. Sutro also knew that the mining companies would have to pay well to use his tunnel.

His vision earned him the sobriquet "Crazy Sutro," but the famed Sutro Tunnel nonetheless emerged from this ambitious dream. Joseph Aron, one of Sutro's friends who financially supported Leah and the six children in San Francisco, said that, "Judging by his actions, [the Tunnel] was more sacred to him than his marriage vows…" He was right. Sutro had found his mistress. On October 31, 1864, Nevada became the 36th state. Sutro petitioned the newly seated state Legislature for a right-of-way to build his tunnel. Mine owners, stockholders and bankers worried that Sutro would take over the Comstock once his tunnel was completed. He ran into resistance at every turn. No one in California or Nevada would invest the capital needed to fund the project. But Sutro wouldn't quit and over time he acquired congressional support and financial investors. Despite his indomitable will and considerable persuasive powers, the four-mile-long tunnel took nine years and $6.5 million to complete. It was a small price to pay, considering that during the bulk of those years, the Comstock produced nearly $309 million in silver and gold. Unfortunately, by the time the Sutro Tunnel reached the vertical mining shafts, the Comstock mines as a group were already in decline. But Sutro was no fool, and shortly after the epic project was finished, he sold all his tunnel stock. Derided as "the Great Bore" early on, "Crazy Sutro" quietly pocketed nearly $1 million in profit. After twenty years of hard, passionate work, his love affair with Nevada's Comstock Lode was over.

San Francisco was in bad economic straits when Sutro returned to his wife and children in 1881. Land values were low, real estate sales sluggish and less than half the city occupied. Sutro's mission on the Comstock was complete; it was time to focus his exceptional energy on the struggling city he loved. He invested his Tunnel profit in San Francisco real estate. Sutro bought thousands of acres between downtown San Francisco and the ocean, a treeless expanse of shifting sand dunes which was also considered another Sutro folly. But over the next fifteen years, Sutro the philanthropist built some of San Francisco's most famous landmarks. He utilized classical Greek statues and urns, transplanted trees and manicured lawns to transform the wild bluffs overlooking the Pacific Ocean into the magnificent Sutro

Heights. Among the famous visitors who joined Sutro at the Heights was President Benjamin Harrison, who feasted on a sumptuous lunch there in 1891. The menu featured California oysters, roast chicken and duck, five different wines, an 1825 cognac and, of course, fine cigars.

Sutro Heights was not reserved for the rich and famous. Sutro the socialist wanted to provide wholesome entertainment for the masses, so he opened his gardens free to the public in 1885. To help more families enjoy the bounty of the Pacific tidewater, Sutro constructed a large natural aquarium north of Fisherman's Cove. At the time, the Cliff House was famous for its wild parties and social deviance from Victorian Society. Its racy reputation was confirmed when rumors flared that women were actually drinking alcohol and smoking cigars at the all-night binges. After an explosion that was caused by a hidden cache of dynamite, a local clergyman claimed the destruction was the hand of God. Infatuated with the seals that basked on the offshore rocks, Sutro bought the seedy Cliff House and transformed it into a respectable family resort. To help families with young children travel to the Cliff House, he built his own streetcar line and charged only a nickel to ride.

Together with the famous poet Joaquin Miller, he planned California's first Arbor Day. On November 27, 1886, Sutro the conservationist went with a large group of state officials to barren Yerba Buena Island and planted thirty thousand trees. Over the years it is estimated Sutro provided San Francisco schoolchildren with hundreds of thousands of fir, eucalyptus and cypress seedlings which he imported from Australia and near the Black Sea. The fish and frolicking seals in his aquarium gave Sutro another idea.

The Sutro Baths were his last great public building project. Opened in 1894, the complex was an enormous glass pavilion enclosing six saltwater swimming pools and one freshwater tank. The largest tank was kept at ocean temperature, but the five other pools, aligned in a row, were steam-heated to progressively warmer temperatures. It also contained three restaurants, five hundred private dressing rooms and a tiered grandstand that seated fifty-three hundred spectators. The baths accommodated ten thousand people at one time; an on-site laundry could wash twenty thousand swimsuits and forty thousand towels a day. Besides swimming meets and musical concerts, there were exhibitions such as a canine named Jack, billed as "the highest diving dog in the world." Sutro often offered free admission for schoolchildren. Tough as steel in business but unfailingly generous to the less fortunate, Sutro expressed hope that the baths "would provide health-giving amusement" and give visitors an advantage in the "struggles of life."

Adolph Sutro died in San Francisco on August 8, 1898, at age sixty-eight. Only a few friends attended the Jewish service that was led by a rabbi who stated that Sutro was "one of the most striking figures in the procession of personages that has made the history of the Pacific Slope." Throughout his life, Sutro was blessed with great physical energy. He firmly believed that fresh air, recreation and frequent bathing were the keys to good health. A hero to the Comstock miners and benevolent benefactor for San Francisco's working class, Adolph Sutro helped open the West with generosity and grand vision.

CHAPTER NINE SELECTED SOURCES

Mary and Robert Stewart, *Adolph Sutro: A Biography,* Howell–North, Berkeley, CA,1962.

Eliot Lord, *Comstock Mining and Miners,* 1883, reprinted by Howell–North, Berkeley, CA, 1959.

U.S. Geological Survey Monograph IV, 47th Congress, 1st Session, House of Representatives Documents, Vol. 16, Washington, DC, 1881.

Grant H. Smith, *History of the Comstock Lode, 1850 – 1920,* State Bureau of Mines, University of Nevada, Reno, Nevada, 1943.

Myron Angel, *History of Nevada,* 1882, reprinted by Howell–North, Berkeley, CA, 1958.

Eugenia Kellogg Homes, *Adolph Sutro,* Press of San Francisco Photo-Engraving Co., 1895.

George D. Lyman, *Ralston's Ring: California Plunders the Comstock Lode,* Scribner's Sons, New York, NY, 1937.

Donald Dale Jackson, *One Man's Soaring Stately Pleasure Dome for the People,* article in *Smithsonian Magazine,* February 1993.

Honorable Thomas Wren, *A History of the State of Nevada,* The Lewis Publishing Company, New York, NY, 1904.

Hubert Howe Bancroft, *History of Nevada, Colorado, and Wyoming 1540 – 1888, Vol. XXV,* The History Company, Publishers, San Francisco, CA,

Dan De Quille, *The Big Bonanza,* reprinted by Alfred A. Knopf, New York, NY, 1947.

Sam P. Davis, *The History of Nevada, Vol. I,* The Elms Publishing Co., Reno, Nevada, 1913.

Doreen Chaky, *Sutro's Sensational Tunnel,* article in *Wild West Magazine,* December, 1997.

Earl Pomeroy, *The Pacific Slope: A History of California, Oregon, Washington, Idaho, Utah, and Nevada,* University of Nebraska Press, Lincoln, Nebraska, 1965.

George D. Lyman, *The Saga of the Comstock Lode,* Charles Scribner's Sons, New York NY, 1934.

Lucius Beebe & Charles Clegg, *San Francisco's Golden Era: A Picture Story of San Francisco Before the Fire,* Howell-North, Berkeley, CA, 1960.

Lucius Beebe & Charles Clegg, Steamcars To The Comstock, *Howell-North, Berkeley, CA, 1957.*

San Francisco Daily Alta Californian, *July 13, 1866.*

San Francisco Chronicle & San Francisco Examiner, numerous articles from the 19th & 20th centuries.

Las Vegas Review-Journal, July 30, 1984.

Virginia City *Territorial Enterprise,* August, September, & October, 1869;

Carson City Daily Appeal, October 21, 1869.

PHOTO CREDITS

Page 99   Mining the Comstock, *Frank Leslie's Illustrated Newspaper,* March 9, 1878, by T. de Thulstrup.

Page 103   Adolph Sutro, *Courtesy California Historical Society.*

Sam Brown & Tom Bell: Sierra Bad Men

Like most villains, Sam Brown was a coward. Brown liked to kill, but only when he was empowered by drink and his victim unarmed. In the great battle at Pyramid Lake in 1860, Sam Brown had mustered in with Major Ormsby's Carson City Rangers, riding a great white mare. When fierce Paiute warriors routed the regiments, Sam Brown's horse was shot out from under him. At the same time, Joseph Baldwin was hit by rifle fire and thrown from his mule. Although woozy from his wounds, Baldwin managed to climb back up onto his mount. But before Baldwin could go far, Sam Brown leaped onto the overloaded animal and spurred it on. When Joe became too dizzy to hang on, Brown threw him into the sagebrush and fled for his life.

Instead of standing to face the enemy, Brown had used his great strength to spur the poor mule across one hundred miles of desert and was the second man in from the battlefield. While some of the young men bravely sacrificed themselves to save their comrades, Brown had deserted his company when the Paiute's returned fire. His commander, Major Ormsby, pierced by arrows, had fallen from his mule seriously wounded, but Brown was already fleeing back to the safety of Virginia City. The drunken bravado he displayed so frequently against innocent citizens had been replaced in battle with blatant fear and cowardice.

When Sam Brown swaggered down the street, he was given wide berth. Of medium height and heavy-set, Brown had a florid complexion, coarse red hair, and long whiskers. Some called him "long-haired Sam." He was usually armed with a huge Bowie knife tucked into his belt and a large revolver. When Brown selected his "man for breakfast," it was always someone unarmed and without friends. Sam Brown didn't want anyone coming back for revenge. Brown arrived in Nevada some time in the late 1850s. His brutish reputation had preceded him. Although the official record shows that Sam killed only three men, he was guilty of many more murders. His first victim was a man in Texas, and in 1853 he stabbed a Mr. Lyons to death in Mariposa, California. Sam Brown's murderous behavior forced him to keep moving. While living in the Sierra Nevada gold diggings in 1854, he killed three men from Chile, for which he was sentenced to San Quentin for two years. Shortly after his arrival in Nevada, he murdered a man known as "one-eyed Gray." In 1859, Nevada was still part of the Utah Territory and had no local government or real law enforcement. Nor did vigilante committees such as the "601" make any move to punish Sam Brown, because the men he had killed so far were considered desperados by the community.

Sam spent the harsh winter of 1859-60 holed up in Genoa. It was during that spring that he participated in the Pyramid Lake Indian War. For the next year or so he moved between Genoa and Virginia City, drinking in the saloons and intimidating the populace. On his birthday in July 1861, Sam Brown was celebrating in the barrooms of Carson City. After several hours of serious drinking, Brown and his friend Alexander Henderson set out for Aurora. Sam Brown had decided that since it was his birthday, he must "have a man for supper." On the road to Aurora, the two men stopped at Webster's Hotel, between Carson City and Genoa. Brown picked a quarrel with Mr. Webster, but the hotel owner was packing a pistol, so Sam and Alex backed down and left. Brown was itching for a fight, so he tried the same game with Robert Lockridge in Genoa. But Lockridge, too, was armed and ready to call Brown's bluff. Once again, Brown and Henderson were sent on their way, still spoiling for a killing.

Three miles up the road from Genoa was a hotel owned by Henry Van Sickle, a German rancher and an old resident of the valley. Van Sickle had a reputation for being quiet and easygoing. Sam and his companion figured the mellow rancher would be a risk-free murder. The drunken duo rode up just as the hotel bell was ringing for supper. Sam Brown had been to the hotel many times and had always behaved himself and never provoked a fight. When Henry Van Sickle saw Sam get down from his mount, he politely asked him if he wanted the horse put in the stable. Sporting his loaded revolver, Sam turned to him and said roughly, "No, I am not stopping here, but I have come to kill you!" Before Brown could shoot, Van Sickle darted into the dining-room packed with guests enjoying supper. Sam pursued his victim into the hotel, gun in hand. The terrified patrons instinctively jumped to their feet, effectively covering Van Sickle's escape. Brown angrily holstered his pistol without firing a shot, mounted his horse and resumed his murderous mission.

But Mr. Van Sickle was not going to let the villain get away with threatening him; he didn't want to spend the rest of his days wondering if Sam Brown was going to have him for supper. Van Sickle quickly grabbed his double-barreled shotgun. It was loaded with fine shot for duck hunting, so he added a charge of buckshot to each barrel. He saddled his fastest horse and chased after the rogue criminal. The hotel owner caught up with Brown and Henderson about a mile up the road. Henry yelled for Henderson to get out of the way, which he did readily, and then blasted both barrels at Sam Brown. The explosion knocked Brown off his horse, but failed to injure him seriously. Still, the attack put the fear of God into Brown; he jumped back into the saddle and took off. Like an avenging angel, mild-mannered Henry Van Sickle recklessly chased Brown with his empty gun.

Meanwhile, several guests had followed Van Sickle from the hotel. They brought emotional support and, more importantly, a supply of ammunition. Van Sickle reloaded his gun and flushed the terrified murderer out of a house where he had hidden. Brown barely kept ahead of the determined hotel-owner until finally Van Sickle overtook Brown near Mottsville. Once again Mr. Van Sickle fired both barrels and again he missed. Brown returned fire with three harmless shots at the pursuing German hosteler and then took refuge in Mrs. Mott's farmhouse. Later, under cover of darkness, Brown fled up the road.

Van Sickle refused to let him go, so he rode on to Luther Olds' Hotel, expecting to find Sam already there. But Sam had not come in, so Henry Van Sickle waited outside in the dark. It wasn't long before Van Sickle heard the jingle of Brown's spurs. He caught Brown just as he alighted from his horse. The fearless rancher carefully leveled the shotgun, and when Brown was within point blank range, Van Sickle blurted out, "Sam, I have got you now!" Caught completely by surprise, Sam Brown was riveted with mortal fear. His horrible scream was cut short when two charges of buckshot blew his head off.

Sam Brown was killed on his birthday, July 6, 1861. An inquest was held the next day, but instead of a prison sentence, the coroner's jury felt that Henry Van Sickle deserved a reward for the killing. The jury's verdict was that Samuel Brown had come to his death from "a just dispensation of an all-wise Providence."

Sam Brown was a violent renegade, but just one in a long line of drifters who made the Sierra gold country their personal hunting grounds for murder or money. In the early 1850s, the miners toiling in the foothill diggings were honest men. Yes, there were gamblers and thieves, gunfights and stabbings, but stealing gold was considered taboo. Bands of highway robbers might waylay an individual traveler, but none had dared to rob a stagecoach of the golden treasure it carried.

The long peace was shattered when Tom Bell and his gang attempted California's first stage robbery. On August 11, 1856, the bold bandits stopped the Camptonville-Marysville stage, intent on plundering $100,000 in gold from the money box of Langton's Pioneer Express Company. Sam W. Langton had established his stage company in Downieville, California, in February 1850. For six years, Langton's Express Co. had transported gold and passengers safely and securely, covering the region from the Bear River to the north fork of the Yuba River, a territory which included Nevada County. But Bell and his boys had broken the public trust, and Californians were outraged. News of the hold-up spread like wildfire. Fact and fancy were mixed in equal parts. Bell's reputation as a cattle rustler and road agent had preceded this latest crime, but within a few weeks, he became a legend.

The *Sacramento Union* newspaper reported, "Tom Bell carries six revolvers and several Bowie knives, and wears a breastplate of thin boiler-iron around his body." The correspondent also predicted that Bell would one day find himself at the end of a rope. Another sensationalist journalist described Tom Bell as a strapping, ferocious fellow, ready to shoot on sight. Other people claimed that Bell was a gentle man, ready to assist those in need. It was already well known that when one of his men shot someone who refused to surrender his moneybelt, Tom Bell had tended to the victim's wound and sent the man to a doctor. But it became more disconcerting when still other men said that they had known Tom Bell as a miner near Rough and Ready, California. They said he was a small, quiet man, neither a bandit bristling with weapons nor a sympathetic nurse who healed wounded travelers. The true identity of Tom Bell was a mystery.

In fact, there was no mystery, but it took Sierra lawmen years to figure it all out. The Tom Bell in this story was really Dr. Thomas J. Hodges, a brilliant Alabama-born surgeon. Hodges had served as a medical attaché with a regiment of Tennessee Volunteers who marched on Mexico in the Mexican-American War of 1846. Little is known of Dr. Hodges' performance in the war, but somehow his nose was badly broken "dented in at the bridge, level with his face." After the military campaign, Dr. Hodges traveled to the Sierra mining districts. No one knows whether Dr. Hodges practiced medicine in California, but he certainly tried his hand at mining and gambling.

When he failed in those pursuits, Hodges' traded in his medical degree for two six-guns and a life of crime. Dr. Hodges was arrested for looting a San Francisco cabin in 1855. When the county peace officers asked for his name, "Tom Bell" was his response. Hodges had heard of a small-time cattle thief by that name who worked the Sierra foothills. If the doctor-turned-criminal told the sheriff his real name, it was likely that he would receive a long sentence for the other crimes he had recently committed, so he used the alias. Confusing the law officers now might help him in the future. The doctor was convicted as "Tom Bell" and incarcerated on Angel Island in San Francisco Bay. In prison Hodges met Bill Gristy, alias "Bill White," who had been sentenced to ten years for stealing three horses from the Girard House in Placer County. He also befriended Ned Connor, a fierce-looking bandit and

Jim Smith, an escape artist whose body was covered with tattoos. These men would later make up the core of Hodges' gang. Hodges began scheming his escape as soon as the cell door slammed shut.

Within a couple of weeks, prisoner "Bell" was feigning a severe illness. There was no doctor on Angel Island and Warden Jack Hayes was worried that Bell would die. He was evacuated to San Francisco where the city physician could examine the "dying" convict. Hodges' medical experience helped convince the doctor that he really was ill. For health reasons, Tom Bell was "granted the privilege of exercise with extended liberties." He took full advantage of the term "extended liberties" and quickly escaped. Months later, Gristy, Connor, and Smith, along with several other men, escaped from Angel Island in a mass prison break. "Tom Bell" and the escaped prisoners rendezvoused in the Sierra and joined forces. To organize their gang, the hardened criminals recruited a dozen other tough characters.

The gang members split into small groups and began terrorizing the foothill communities north of Auburn. No crime was too insignificant for this gang. They stole cattle and robbed travelers; they burglarized stores and rumbled in saloons. But no matter where or how they broke the law, they made sure that their victims believed that it was "Tom Bell" doing the dirty work. This plan to confuse the general public worked well. To the average citizen it appeared that Bell and his gang could rob a traveler in one part of the county, and on the same day, bust up a saloon two hundred miles away. No horse could travel that fast. Sheriffs spent all their time chasing the phantom Tom Bell from county to county. For law enforcement, it was a frustrating game of cat and mouse.

Meanwhile, Tom Bell was relaxing at the Mountaineer House, between Folsom and Auburn. The Mountaineer House was owned by Jack Phillips, a convict from Australia who had brought his criminal lifestyle to California. It was the perfect hangout for Bell and his gang. Every so often peace officers heard that Bell was drinking at Phillips' saloon, but by the time they arrived, Bell would be gone and Jack Phillips would be at his desk quietly checking paperwork. The only customers at the bar were always just the stagecoach driver and his weary passengers, who had stopped for a drink before tackling the steep, dusty road to Nevada City. For months Bell stayed one step ahead of the law, but bit by bit local deputies gathered details about the elusive bandit. County sheriffs exchanged letters and networked their information. Officers were soon on the look-out for Bell's broken nose, a facial feature difficult to hide in public. They learned that he was tall and broad-shouldered, with a thin, wiry build. Bell was known to have a quick temper and was considered fearless in a fight. Informants also told peace officers that Tom Bell had long blond hair, and was vain about his trimmed and manicured whiskers. Sierra lawmen could finally distinguish the real Tom Bell from his imposters, but could they catch the crafty criminal?

The Bell & White gang continued to prey on anyone they caught on the road. No one was safe, not even the local miners or merchants. In the spring of 1856, freight driver Dutch John was hauling a cargo of beer to the small community of Drytown, but the bandits weren't thirsty. The highwaymen grabbed his $30, returned some change, and then told poor John to buy himself a drink when he got to town. Despite the bold and frequent hold-ups, lawmen seemed helpless in their efforts to catch Bell and his boys. Ordinary citizens were getting fed up with the rampant robberies. Mr. Woods was the toll collector for a bridge on the south fork of the Yuba River. One day three horsemen rode past him without paying, saying that Tom Bell's gang didn't pay toll to anyone. The *San Francisco Bulletin* reported Woods' reaction to this piracy: "Mr. Woods is not the man to take this kind of thing lying down. He rushed back to his house, grabbed his rifle and fired several shots at the three. He pursued them as far as French Corral. A company started in pursuit and pressed the men so hard that one was forced to dismount and take to the scrub. The course of the robbers was seen to be up the ridge, but the trail grew cold and they were not caught." Once again, the elusive bandits had escaped.

Despite his success as a road agent, Tom Bell grew weary of his small-time hits on teamsters and beer merchants. No highway robber had yet waylaid a stagecoach carrying the gold-laden Wells Fargo treasure chest, so he decided to be the first. While planning this big heist, Bell reined in his henchmen. With Bell's gangsters off the road, the summer of 1856 was unusually quiet in the mining country. Relieved citizens and wary lawmen both assumed that Tom Bell had fled to another part of the country. The temporary lull in crime ended with a bang when in August 1856, Bell and his gang accosted the Camptonville stage, packed with passengers and $100,000 in gold dust. The bags of gold were owned by Mr. Rideout, a gold dealer in Camptonville. No one had ever robbed a California stage before and there was an armed guard sitting next to the driver, but Rideout had decided he'd rather be safe than sorry. The prudent but un-armed gold merchant rode his horse out in front of the stage, ahead of the choking dust. Later that afternoon, Mr. Rideout took a little-used fork in the road along Dry Creek, spooking three masked men hidden in the brush. Rideout carried no weapon, so the armed men on horseback ordered him to dismount. After searching his pockets and taking the horse, the foolish bandits let the frightened merchant go free. Rideout scurried across the ravine and climbed up to the main road just ahead of the coach. Before he could shout a warning, gunfire erupted in the hot afternoon air. Tom Bell and two masked men had ambushed the stage.

Bell's well-laid plan had called for six armed men on horseback, three on each side of the stage, but Mr. Rideout's appearance had ruined their careful timing. With the attack coming from only one direction, the armed guard was able to blast one bandit with his first shot. At that, Bell and his men opened fire, riddling the stage with bullets. Several passengers inside the coach produced their own weapons, and a fire-fight ensued. Some forty shots were fired within the first two minutes. By then, Bell and his wounded men had retreated to the safety of the brush, at which point the stage raced towards Marysville. Just then the three delayed gang members galloped up the road with Rideout's horse in tow. Despite a bullet wound in his right arm, the guard was ready for them, too. He took a fast shot and sent the lead rider tumbling dead into the dust. The other riders scrambled. In the confusion, Mr. Rideout was able to grab his horse and raced off after the speeding stagecoach. Tom Bell's carefully-planned hold-up had failed to get the gold, but there was no cause for celebration. The armed-guard was not the only person hurt. Many of the passengers suffered gunshot wounds, one man in the shoulder and another in both legs. Mrs. Tilghman, a black women and wife of a Marysville barber, had been shot through the head and killed instantly. Since Mrs. Tilghman was black, she had been forced to ride on an outside back seat of the stage with several Chinese. She was hit in the first volley.

The next day, details of the brutal crime headlined the *Marysville Express* newspaper. The entire countryside was up in arms for Bell's capture, but the gangster was unrepentant.

In a letter to the newspaper, Bell wrote that he refused to give up, and taunted the populace with "catch me if you can." The chase was on. One by one, Bell's gang members were caught or killed. Finally, in early October, a posse led by Judge Belt ambushed Tom Bell at his secluded hideout at Firebaugh's Ferry near the San Joaquin River. A rider was sent for the sheriff, but when it came to justice for the murderous Bell, Judge Belt had little faith in the due process of law. The vigilantes had no idea that Bell's true identity was really, Dr. Thomas J. Hodges, but it didn't matter anyway. They had the right man. The twenty-six-year-old highwayman was given just enough time to write a letter to his mother. He wrote, *"Dear Mother, As I am about to make my exit to another country, I take this opportunity to write you a few lines. Though my fate has been a cruel one, yet I have no one to blame but myself. Give my respects to all my old and youthful friends. Tell them to beware of bad associations, and never to enter into any gambling saloons, for that has been my ruin. Probably you may never hear from me again. If not, I hope that we may meet where parting is no more."* Hodges had spared his mother the pain of knowing her son was a murderer. Ten minutes later, "Tom Bell" was swinging from a hemp rope, his life just another footnote in Sierra history.

CHAPTER TEN SELECTED SOURCES

Myron Angel, *History of San Luis Obispo County, California,* Thompson and West, 1883, reprinted by Howell-North Books, Berkeley, CA, 1966,

Rudolph M. Lapp, *Blacks in Gold Rush California,* Yale University Press, New Haven, Connecticut, 1977.

Bill O'Neal, *Encyclopedia of Western Gunfighters,* University of Oklahoma Press, Norman, OK, 1979.

Frank T. Gilbert, *History of San Joaquin County, California,* Thompson and West, 1879, reprinted by Howell–North Books, Berkeley, CA, 1968.

R.E. Mather & F.E. Boswell, *Gold Camp Desperadoes: Violence, Crime, and Punishment on the Mining Frontier,* University of Oklahoma Press, Norman, OK, 1993.

Edward B. Scott, *The Saga of Lake Tahoe, vol. 1,* Sierra-Tahoe Publishing Co., Crystal Bay, Lake Tahoe, Nevada, 1957.

Jay Robert Nash, *Encyclopedia of Western Lawmen and Outlaws,* De Capo Press, New York, NY, 1989.

Joseph Henry Jackson, *Bad Company: The Story of California Stage-Robbers, Bandits & Highwaymen,* Harcourt Brace, New York, NY, 1949.

George D. Lyman, *The Saga of the Comstock Lode,* Charles Scribner's Sons, New York, NY, 1934.

PHOTO CREDITS

Page 113   Bandit Hideout, *Frank Leslie's Illustrated Newspaper,* March 23, 1890, by A.C. Redwood.

If you enjoyed reading *Sierra Stories — True Tales of Tahoe*, and would like information about other exciting books and dramatic stories on audio cassette tape, please contact Mic Mac Publishing. The author, Mark McLaughlin, is available for entertaining presentations on authentic western history and spellbinding storytelling.

Mic Mac
Publishing

P. O. Box 483 • Carnelian Bay, CA 96140
Phone/Fax: (530) 546-5612

Books and Tapes

PERFECT GIFTS FOR ANY OCCASION!

Sierra Stories — Autographed Books
    ☐ Volume 1   ☐ Volume 2
☐ Donner Party Audio Tape
☐ Nevada Weather Stories Audio Tape

Please enclose check for $9.95 + $2.00 S&H per item
(California residents add 7.25% sales tax)

Mail check and address info to:
    P. O. Box 483, Carnelian Bay, CA 96140

Please make checks payable to Mark McLaughlin

Name: _____

Address: _____

City: _____ State: _____ Zip: _____